IF TuNa COULd KiLL

IF Tuna Could Kill

The Capers of Cobalt Bay - Book 2

BY

If Tuna Could Kill
Capers of Cobalt Bay, Book 2

Published by Pacific Lights Publishing
Copyright © 2023 by Trinity Colt. All rights reserved.

Cover design by Lynnette Bonner of Indie Cover Design, images ©
www.depositphotos.com, File: # 41260981 – café
www.depositphotos.com, File: # 53301825 – cat
www.depositphotos.com, File: # 49616621 – scene through window
www.depositphotos.com, File: # 265378930 – body outline

Paperback ISBN: 978-1-942982-29-6

Something Fishy

"I CAN'T BELIEVE THIS is happening!" My friend, Belinda Cooke, paced the tiles between the massive commercial ovens and the huge mixing bowl in the corner of her bakery's kitchen. Her hands hadn't stopped wringing since I'd snuck in the back door of Just Desserts a few minutes ago.

Tuna, the Cookes' massive marmalade tabby cat, meowed as if in agreement with Belinda's lament. I still wasn't certain how I felt about a cat having free roam in a bakery, but I had never said anything to Belinda, and now certainly wasn't the time to bring it up—not with her son's best friend lying dead in the next room with a knife in his back.

I eased the swinging doors open a spare inch and peered into the front of the bakery. And okay, yes, here I'll admit that I was doing my best to stay out of the line of sight of one Sheriff Elijah Gains.

When he'd gotten the call about this murder, we'd been on a date that apparently wasn't a date—long story. Fine—maybe not so long. I'd thought it was a date, but Elijah had made it clear he saw it only as two friends going for coffee, which was a bit of a let-down, if I was honest. On the other hand, he had then asked me on a "real" date, but I hadn't gotten the chance to answer before he'd taken the call about this murder.

Elijah had told his deputy, Auggy, to take me home. But Auggy was a pushover and it hadn't taken much persuasion to change that plan.

However, one officer was not exactly like the other. Elijah definitely wasn't a pushover and would not be happy if he caught sight of me here at his crime scene. Especially since I'd recently nearly gotten myself killed by poking into his last case—but really, what was I supposed to do when a coffin had washed up on my beach? And if I hadn't done some poking around of my own, Randall Creeper, the former Cobalt Bay mortician-turned-murderer, might still be roaming free.

My stomach turned a little sick. I wrapped my clammy arms around myself.

I honestly had learned my lesson—nearly dying will do that to a girl. I didn't plan to stick my nose into any more of Elijah's cases, thank you very much. However, I couldn't leave my friend Belinda on her own when somebody had just dropped dead in her bakery, which was why I'd talked Auggy into letting me in through the back door—so I could comfort her.

I nudged the butler doors open a little more.

On the other side of the bakery display case, Elijah and Undersheriff Jason White stood by the window that looked over the bay. They both had their attention fixed on the floor near their feet as they spoke in hushed tones. The counter prevented me from being able to see the floor, but from what Belinda had babbled to me over the last few minutes, there was apparently a dead body at their feet. Duke and his son, who I hadn't yet met, sat glumly at a table against the far wall. Both stared morosely into space, hands folded before them.

I narrowed my eyes at the son. I couldn't really see his face from this angle. Was he cold-blooded enough to stab his supposed best friend and then stroll into his parents' bakery like nothing had happened? Knowing Duke and Belinda, it wasn't likely they'd raised such a son; however nothing should be overlooked, so it warranted some consideration.

Behind me, Belinda continued to pace and wring.

"Here." I nudged her toward the chair at the little shabby-chic accounting desk in the corner. "Sit. Let me get you some coffee." I wanted to soothe her distress as she had on so many occasions for me with one of her chocolate croissants. Maybe getting her to talk would help.

As I hefted the Bunn carafe and poured her a mug of the steaming black liquid, I glanced at her. "Tell me again how you knew him." I swung a nod toward the front of the store where the corpse was still being photographed and studied by Elijah and his law-enforcement officers.

I would reserve judgment about her son until I could learn more about the situation.

Belinda absentmindedly accepted the cup I slid her way. "He and Garrett, our son, grew up together here on the island. They both are in town for the fishing tournament that starts tomorrow. We were so happy that we were going to have them home for a few days . . ."

"What's his name?" I laid my hand against her forearm and gave it a squeeze.

"Tony—Anthony. Anthony Moretti." Her posture sagged even more. "He's only in his twenties. I can't imagine what his parents are going to feel when they find out."

"Do they still live here on the island?"

She shook her head. "They moved several years back after Tony and Garrett graduated. I think they are in Seattle now."

"And what happened exactly?" I'd been trying to wrap my brain around her disjointed chatter but hadn't been able to get a clear picture of the events that had transpired. Elijah and I had literally been on our non-date less than twenty minutes ago and everything had been fine. Maybe if I could get her to start from the beginning . . . "Elijah and I were just here." I returned the carafe to the hotplate.

She nodded. "This morning Garrett and Tony took our boat out to make sure everything was in good working order before tomorrow. Duke and I haven't had much time to go boating, lately. They were going to do a little fishing and then meet us here. We planned to do a fish-fry at our place for dinner this evening."

I nodded encouragingly. This telling of the story was much more coherent than her last.

Belinda took a sip of coffee, then propped her head into one hand. "Just after you and Elijah left, Garrett came into the bakery."

"Alone?" I felt the tension of a frown between my brows. She'd said so earlier, but I wanted to confirm.

Belinda nodded.

"And he seemed normal?" This bit of information I had also gathered from her earlier rendition.

"Yes. Garrett said they'd made a good catch this morning. They were on their way here, but Tony saw an old friend and told Garrett he would be along in just a few minutes." Her hand trembled against the desk calendar.

I reached over the table to grip it. "You don't have to tell me more, if you don't want to." I said the words, but hoped she wouldn't take me up on the offer. I was dying to know what had happened. Sorry! I know! I'm terrible. In my defense, all I'll say is that my friend Colleen's ability to crack bad puns has apparently rubbed off on me.

"It's okay." Belinda brought me back to the present as she blew on her cup and took another sip. "Duke and Garrett each grabbed a donut and had just sat down at one of the tables out front. I was at the sink, cleaning up some dishes." A short gesture directed my attention toward the double-bowled stainless-steel monstrosity of a commercial sink against one wall. The sprayer faucet dangled in mid-air above a large mixing bowl that lay in one basin, evidence that Belinda had been interrupted mid-rinse.

Belinda closed her eyes and pressed her lips together.

I felt guilty for wanting her to continue. I forced myself to do the right thing. "I should go—"

"No. It's okay." She straightened. "Maybe talking about it will help me get the vision of it out of my head. I was at the sink when I heard Duke and Garrett yelling from the front. I hurried out there. But by the time I got there, Tony had collapsed onto the floor. There was a knife in his back." She shivered and rubbed her hands against her arms. Tears glimmered in her eyes. "They said he kept saying, 'I didn't take it. Tell them I didn't take it.'"

"Didn't take what?"

She shook her head. "None of us knows what he was talking about. He and Garrett had only been apart for a few minutes at that point. And Garrett said the only person they saw was someone Tony knew on the boat a few slips down."

"Garrett didn't know the person?"

Belinda frowned. Twisted her mug. "I don't know, to be honest. Everything just happened so fast. None of us have really had a chance to talk."

"I understand. I'm so sorry. I'm sure Elijah will get this all figured out." And speaking of that man . . . "I really should get out of your hair. Call me if you need anything?"

Belinda clutched at my hand. "There is something you could do, if you don't mind?"

"Sure. Anything."

"Tony had the cooler of fish they caught with him."

Uh-oh. My focus flashed to the swinging door between us and the dining area.

Belinda was still talking. "He dropped it by the front door when he stumbled in. The fish are on ice, but I'm afraid if we don't get them gutted and frozen right away, they're going to go bad. I don't see us having the time or energy to grill them tonight."

I swallowed. Anything but that. Was this the time to admit that I had no idea how to gut a fish and absolutely no desire to learn? Or the time to admit that I couldn't let Elijah see me here?

One glance at Belinda, with her hands over her face as she pressed a tissue to her eyes, had me stepping toward the swinging door. "Sure. Not a problem."

Liar, liar, pants on fire.

But how hard could gutting a fish be? I cringed. And that wasn't even my biggest problem.

First, I had to make it past Elijah.

I poked my head through the swinging doors and then bravely strode along the gray-tiled floor behind the counter like I was supposed to be here. Elijah still stood at the far end of the room, focused on the floor. Jason now spoke quietly to Duke and Garrett at their table. Auggy seemed to be arranging some equipment on one of the tables behind Elijah.

Just as I rounded the end of the counter, Elijah's focus snapped to me.

I froze.

"What are you doing here?" His words held genuine surprise, proving that he really hadn't realized I was in the kitchen.

Auggy jolted upright and gaped at me over Elijah's shoulder. He gave me a wide-eyed subtle shake of his head.

Right. Don't throw Auggy under the bus. I clutched my hands in front of myself, doing my best to ignore the black rubber booted foot of the corpse on the floor. "Uh, I was just with Belinda in the kitchen."

Auggy dropped the little stack of numbered crime scene markers he was holding. They clattered all over the floor. He scrambled after them.

When he was once more on his feet, the look Elijah pegged him with could have shattered steel.

"Sorry, boss," Auggy mumbled, head hanging.

Elijah shuffled. That telltale muscle bunched in his jaw. His gaze drilled into mine, even as he spoke to his deputy. "Sorry for dropping those all over my crime scene? Or sorry for letting Shelby into the kitchen earlier?"

Uh-oh. Busted. My focus slipped to the tip of one of Elijah's black Vans. He was still in his civilian attire, which he'd been wearing on our non-date, and I tried not to think about how fine those ripped jeans looked on him. I failed.

Poor Auggy hefted the camera that dangled from his neck. "Uh, boss, I really should go process these pictures back at the station so's they'll be ready when you want to study them."

"All right. Go on then."

Looking relieved, Auggy scrambled toward the bakery's front door.

"But Auggy?" A twinkle of humor glinted in Elijah's gaze that was still pinned to mine.

Auggy lurched to a stop, one hand on the door handle. "Yeah, boss?"

"Don't ever let an interloper into one of my crime scenes again, understand?"

The deputy's mouth opened, and I could tell he wanted to argue that he hadn't really let me into the crime scene, but one glance from Elijah in his direction, and he snapped it shut again so quickly that I heard his teeth clack. "Yes, boss."

Elijah gave him a nod and Auggy surged from the room like a chicken freed from a slaughterhouse.

"Interloper?" I plunked my hands on my hips.

Elijah's gaze once more drilled into mine. He ignored my accusation. "What can I do for you, Shel?"

Oh, I liked the way he said that shortened form of my name a lot, but the weariness that weighted his shoulders raised my concern.

I forgot for the moment about the cooler of fresh fish I was to collect. I only wanted to comfort him. I took a step forward, but he jutted out a hand to stop me.

"Please. Don't come any closer. We still have to process this." He swept a gesture at the victim.

I swallowed, wishing I could tear my gaze away from the body I could now fully see, but I couldn't seem to find the strength. The man sprawled on the floor wore a hefty winter coat, cargo pants, and the aforementioned black fisherman's boots. The bone hilt of a knife with a bull elk etched into it protruded from the coat just below one shoulder blade. One arm stretched above his head.

Lightheadedness swirled through me.

Elijah stepped over the body and took my arm gently. His voice was soft when he said, "Go back into the kitchen, Shel."

"I . . . Um . . . Sorry. It's just that since my dad passed . . ."

"I know." His voice dropped into a soothing tone that somehow eased my tension. "You're not so good around dead bodies."

His hand was firm on my back as he nudged me forward. When we came even with the gap in the display cases that housed the till, I noticed Tuna perched on the countertop, peering toward the body. I didn't want her to jump down and mess up the crime scene while Elijah was distracted with me, so I scooped her into my arms.

"Come on, Tuna."

Maybe it was the sound of the cat's name that jolted my memory. I looked at Elijah. "I almost forgot. The reason I came out here is that Belinda wants me to clean the fish and put them in the freezer. Is there a cooler out there somewhere?" I tipped a nod to the other side of the display counter.

"Yeah, we already processed it for fingerprints. I'll get it." He motioned for me to go on into the kitchen, then retraced our steps.

I'd barely had time to deposit Tuna into Belinda's lap, where she still sat at the accounting desk, before Elijah pushed through the swinging doors and set the red Coleman on the drainboard by the sink.

He returned to stand near the desk. "You doing okay, Belinda?"

I left them to talk and inched toward the cooler with the speed of a prisoner on death row taking their last walk. I could already smell the stench of little fish corpses.

If only Belinda didn't make such delicious pain au chocolat, maybe I wouldn't like her so much. Then I wouldn't be standing here working up my courage to gut some fish. Sheesh! I didn't even know *how* to gut fish.

I whipped out my phone and cringed my way through a short how-to video. After fetching the sharp knife the video said I needed, I gave the lid of the cooler a tap. This job wasn't going to get any easier if I put it off. How many fish could there be in here, anyhow?

Taking a fortifying breath, I lifted the white hinged lid. Inside, four large fish stared up at me, mouths agape. They looked slimy. And scaley.

Ew. Ew, ew, ew.

Something inside me died a little when I thought about how they'd been swimming contentedly in their vast ocean home and just trying to survive when, *wham*, they swallowed the wrong morsel of food.

I bent closer to the cooler and whispered, "Life can be like that. Sorry you ended up in the wrong place at the wrong time, little fish."

Little? Not so much. I swallowed. Okay, I had to get on with it already.

"Dear Lord Almighty, give me strength," I muttered.

I reached for the top carcass. But it was heavier than I expected, and did I mention slimy? The fish slipped out of my hands and landed in the sink with a loud clatter that sounded like broken glass.

My brow puckered. Broken glass? I leaned forward to peer into the sink. My eyes practically bugged out of my head.

"Uh . . . Elijah? You should see this. I think I just found the motive for Anthony's murder."

A Little Snooping

ELIJAH STOOD SILENTLY BESIDE me as we stared into the sink.

"Are those what I think they are?" I asked.

The large fish lay to one side of the sink, but scattered across the bottom of the stainless basin were crystal clear pieces of square rocks.

Elijah pegged me with a look and boy could his baby blues turn cloudy and menacing when he was on the job. "What did you do?"

My jaw dropped. Of all the—"I didn't *do* anything. Belinda asked me to gut the fish and prep them for the freezer. I took the top one out of the cooler"—I motioned to the red Coleman on the drainboard—"and it slipped out of my hands and those fell out of it."

"You didn't gut it? Because it's been gutted."

If I rolled my eyes it was sheerly a reflex, honest. "I can see that."

"So why were you putting it into the sink?"

"Well, it didn't *look* like it had been gutted before I picked it up." The man really could be exasperating. "I watched a video that showed how to, you know, remove the insides." My lip curled and when humor lit his gaze, I gave him an exaggerated nose-scrunch. "I was going to give it a try. The sink seemed like the best place for that."

"You've never gutted a fish before?"

"Shocking as it may be, the answer is no."

A softness stole into his expression. "But you were willing to do it for the Cookes?"

Belinda still sat in the chair across the room. Her focus seemed to be somewhere very far away, however.

I lowered my voice. "I just wanted to help in any way I could."

Our attention fell to the rocks in the sink once more. Lots of them.

Elijah picked up a fork from the drainboard and pried up one side of the fish so we could see inside it. More rocks filled it.

All told, there were hundreds. Maybe thousands. Some were bigger and less uniform. A lot were smaller and almost exactly square in shape.

Elijah loosed a low whistle. He stepped to the cooler and eyed the three other fish. I was right beside him, on my tiptoes, peering into the depths. And I was pleased to see that I wasn't going crazy because just like the fish in the sink, all these fish appeared to be whole, as well. Using the fork, Elijah prodded at the belly of one of the fish and with a little pressure, a seam split open and the glitter of more stones could be seen.

"Are those diamonds?" I whispered.

"Whatever they are, one bite of this tuna could kill a person. It's certain this catch wasn't meant for eating." Elijah's next words sent disappointment shooting through me. "Shelby, I'm going to have to ask you to step away from the sink. This area just became part of my crime scene."

"Do you think we might get a founder's fee, or something? Maybe we've just busted open a smuggling ring!" I'm not afraid to admit that a thrill of excitement swept through me at the thought. I leaned over the sink to take in all that sparkle again. Just the sight of so much glitter sent my pulse into a double-time rhythm.

But Elijah's withering glower brought me back down to earth.

I raised my palms. "Fine. I know. Stay out of your investigation." I pouted. Motioned toward the door. "I should probably get going anyhow. This weekend will be our first few days where the B&B is sold out."

With Auggy busy back at the station, I wondered how I was going to get home now. Elijah had picked me up at the B&B for our non-date and I didn't have my car. I guessed I'd have to walk.

On instinct I started toward the front, but Elijah grabbed my elbow. "Out the back way like you came in, if you please."

I glared at him, trying to ignore the pleasant sensation of his gentle grip on my arm. "Bye, Belinda. Text me if you need anything," I called as Elijah practically propelled me into the back alley.

I huffed and straightened my jacket. Elijah remained in the doorway, brows lifted. He held out his hand. A fob dangled from his first finger. "You'll have to take my truck. I'll have Auggy give me a ride so I can come get it later. It's parked in front of the bakery, if you recall."

I tucked my lower lip between my teeth. The man was a walking contradiction. First kicking me out, but then being thoughtful enough to remember I didn't have a vehicle nearby. I took the key. "Thanks."

He nodded. Folded his arms. "I'll watch until you turn the corner of the building."

My wrinkled nose and curled lip were probably not the best look I'd ever sported. "Sheesh. You act like I'm going to singlehandedly let the bad guys get away. I just wanted to comfort Belinda. And you wouldn't know about those diamonds yet if it wasn't for me." Would that draw any more information out of him? He still hadn't said whether he even thought the stones were diamonds or not.

All he did was lower his chin, and continue to point in the direction of the alley that would lead me toward his truck out front. "And I just want to keep you safe."

I wanted to gesture to the quaint town surrounding me and ask how much danger I could be in, but with a dead body lying back there in the bakery — and the little incident in recent history where the town's mortician had tried to murder me by locking me in one of his refrigeration drawers — I didn't have much leverage.

"Fine. I'm off."

My waggling fingers ought to have proved my point, but Elijah remained in the doorway, watching me until I turned the corner toward Main Street.

I climbed onto the high running board of his huge black truck, and then slumped into the buttery leather of his driver's seat, feeling the discouragement of the day drooping my shoulders. For all that Elijah might be concerned about my safety, I was also concerned about his. With a murderer in town, the danger of his job had just skyrocketed.

The lovely scent of his cologne enveloped me and I'm not ashamed to tell you that I closed my eyes and pressed my nose against the shoulder of his seat. Mmmm.

I examined the interior of his rig, something I'd been too distracted to do when he picked me up earlier. I was not surprised to find that his truck was immaculate. Not one take-out wrapper littered the floor. All the leather of the dashboard gleamed with a shimmer that showed he kept it polished. Even his floor mats looked like I could eat off them. I made a note that I should clean my car out before I ever gave him a ride anywhere.

I took another look at the bakery, wishing there was something I could do to help him.

But he was right. There really wasn't anything I could do.

Unless . . .

Down the street, a little sliver of the blue waters of the marina peeked from behind the mortuary. A shudder slipped through me. I didn't think I'd ever be able to look at that building without remembering being shut into one of those nasty corpse coolers.

But . . . With a swallow, I shored up my nerves. Thankfully, I wouldn't need to go into the mortuary.

I was just reaching for the door handle, when a loud rapping on the passenger window about launched me into the roof. I pressed one hand to my chest and took a breath.

It was only Belinda peering in at me. She held up a pet crate. Tuna glared at me from inside it with her ears practically pinned to her head.

I pressed the start button on the truck so I could roll the window down. "What's up?" I didn't have a great feeling about this.

"Sorry to startle you. I realized that Tuna shouldn't be wandering the store during the investigation, and I wondered . . . Would you be willing to watch her at the bed and breakfast for . . . I don't know. A few days?"

Just as I'd feared. A few days with a cat? I hoped Belinda couldn't read the reluctance on my face. I really wasn't much of a cat person, though I did like them. Mom loved cats and we'd had two when I was a girl. Both of them had been prone to perching on the tops of doors and taking a swat at passersby. It always sent my heart into my throat.

And forget about my dislike for unexpected whacks from cats' paws. Kodi, my little Pomeranian mix, would go ballistic and then pout for a millennium.

I smiled at Belinda. "Of course. We'd be happy to watch Tuna." I was going to pay for this. I just knew it.

"Thank you so much. I really don't know what I would do without you today. Give me a second to run inside and get the rest of her stuff. Here." She thrust the cat carrier through the open passenger window. "I'll be right back."

As I got Tuna's carrier settled onto the seat and buckled it in, Tuna hissed and growled and mewled.

"Oh, come on. It's not going to be that bad. We'll have fun." I bent down to peer in at her.

She spat and swiped at the gate on the front of her crate with one paw.

I lurched back, whacking my arm on the gearshift. "Ouch!" I rubbed at the spot. "I'll leave you alone. But I hope you are kinder than that to our guests."

Belinda was back. She stuffed a huge fluffy bed through the window. Wow, was Kodi ever going to be jealous of that!

As she shoved things in, I transferred them to Elijah's back seat, and worried whether this was going to reignite Mom's once-yearly-or-so proclamation that we should get a cat.

Tuna's bed was followed by a bin of cat food. "Her bowl and measuring scoop are inside. She gets one scoop in the morning and another at night." Another bin held her toys. And still another bathing supplies. "Sometimes she has . . . issues and needs a bath."

My stomach rolled at the thought of what kind of issue might result in a cat needing a bath. There were too many horrifying images in my mind.

My smile felt like it was chiseled from cement. "I'm sure we'll be fine. We'll take good care of her."

"Oh, and one more thing." She pulled a little bottle filled with clear liquid from her jacket pocket. "She has to take a dose of this every morning. Unfortunately, she hates it. So maybe your mom can help you. Duke usually holds her—with gloves." She paused as though to make sure I'd caught that addendum, then hurried on. "Anyhow, while Duke holds her, I plunge the meds to the back of her throat." She handed me the little bottle and a needleless syringe. "See the line with the two? You fill the syringe to that line and give it to her every morning. You have to make sure she swallows it. It's for her heart."

For some reason, I'd never noticed Belinda's hands before. But after her comment about the gloves, as she reached in to hand me the medicine, my focus settled on her skin. There were long angry red scratches across her knuckles.

Wonderful. What had I gotten myself into? Tuna had always been super sweet to me any time I'd been in the bakery, but clearly there were times when she was more . . . feisty than others.

But maybe something good would come of it. It might make Mom realize that the last thing we needed was a cat.

Belinda tucked her hands into her jacket pockets. "I'd better get back inside. Thanks again, Shelby. You're a doll."

"Not a problem at all." It seemed I was determined to be a liar today. "We can keep her for as long as you need us to." My nose would be breaking the windshield if I wasn't careful.

"Much appreciated. Bye for now." With that, she headed back into the bakery.

Inside her carrier, Tuna yowled.

My gaze settled once more on the marina. "Guess what?" I said to the cat. "You're just the excuse I need. You like fish, don't you? I have just the thing to help you settle in at the B&B."

Somewhere in the time I'd been talking to Belinda, I realized that if I left Elijah's truck parked here near the bakery, he might come out and see it was still here. So this time, instead of reaching for the door handle, I put the Black Beast into gear and backed from my spot. Huh. Being this high up was kind of nice. I could see everything from up here.

It was only two blocks down to the marina parking lot, but there was a nice large van that I parked on the other side of. That should keep the black F250 from being visible from the sidewalk in front of the bakery, should the town's good sheriff decide to step outside.

"I'll be right back, Tuna."

It was a cool, overcast day, and I was parked in the shade of a large madrona, so there wasn't any danger of Tuna overheating, but just as a precaution, I rolled each window down a spare inch. That should give her a little fresh air, at the least. Maybe her mood would be improved by the time I got her home.

I stepped from the truck and locked it behind me. Just a little walk around the marina to buy Tuna some fish—maybe even tuna fish. I giggled. And okay, maybe do a little snooping. After all, it was a very public place, so there was no danger of anyone trying to cram me into a drawer.

Just the thought made my steps falter, but then my mission drove me forward. No one seemed to know who Anthony had stopped to talk to. If I could find that information, maybe it would put Elijah on the right track sooner and bring justice to the man who meant so much to my friends.

A Red Cooler

THE METAL RAMP DOWN to the marina squeaked beneath my Born boots as I stepped onto it. Not the most practical footwear for traipsing around the marina, but less than an hour ago I'd been on my non-date, and a girl had to feel at least a little classy in situations like that. Boots always dressed up a pair of jeans nicely. The heels on this pair weren't too high, so I'd probably be fine.

Midway down the ramp, I paused to take in the chaos that was the marina today. People scurried everywhere, getting ready for tomorrow's big tournament. A man and woman lugged two heavy metal chairs onto a boat and set to screwing them into special receptacles at the stern. Another couple snapped at each other as they attempted to attach a sail to a pole. Pole? Mast? I blew a breath of dismissal. What did I know about boats? About as much as a gator knew about cooking, and that was being generous.

As I stepped onto the main pier, a man hurried by with the biggest fishing rod I'd ever seen resting on his shoulder. I had to duck to avoid getting whacked by the handle. Sheesh. What was he going to catch with that thing? Orcas?

I felt someone watching me and looked toward the building that sat at the center of the marina. It was like the central hub of a wheel and all the docks spoked off from it. "Building" was a little too grand a term. "Shack" was more like it. A cedar shake roof topped wooden-sided walls. The wall closest to me sported a door with a window on either side. To one side of the doorway, a man stood behind a ramped table filled with ice and fish.

"Help you?" He squinted one sun-wrinkled eye. His gray bushy brows arched over a pair of friendly blue eyes—the bluest eyes I'd seen in a long time. I'd bet he was a player in his prime. As if to prove my point, he skimmed me from head to toe in a way that only a man checking out a woman would do.

It could have made me uncomfortable, but somehow the glint in his gaze set me at ease. His scrutiny was more of curiosity than of actual interest.

"You that new owner of the bed and breakfast where poor Mabel ended up?"

It was in that moment that I realized word would certainly reach Elijah that I'd been here. This would likely be his next stop after he finished up at the bakery, and with my fiery red curls, and the fact that

I'd recently been the town's biggest news story since . . . well. . . maybe ever, I wouldn't have any luck keeping the fact that I was here from reaching the sheriff's ears.

I might as well embrace that fact and make the best of it.

Offering my biggest smile, I stepped nearer to his table. "I am." I scanned the poor little fish carcasses on the ice. "I'm here to buy a whole mess of fish for the bed and breakfast. Mom makes the best corn-batter-fried fillets you ever tasted."

"Salmon's fresh caught this morning. But you don't want to go wasting Chinook with corn breading. Do yourself a favor and bake it up with a little salt, dill, and mustard powder. Finish it off with a generous squeeze of lemon. Best fish you ever tasted."

My mouth watered at the thought. I might not be good at gutting and cleaning fish, but I sure was good at eating them. Especially with Mom's home-made tartar sauce.

"Name's Mac Gains." He stretched a bronzed hand across the table.

"Nice to meet you, Mac. I'm Shelby— Gains?"

He chuckled, and in it rang a familiar pattern much like Elijah's.

I tried not to look surprised but had a feeling I failed. Miserably. "Are you . . . related to . . . Sheriff Gains?"

Mac's grin widened. "I'm his grandpa." He gave me another quick sweep. "I can see why he's so taken with you."

"Taken with . . ." Wow. Had a heat wave suddenly blown in on the wind? I gestured to the salmon while reaching for my wallet. "I'll take those four there. Can you wrap them for me?"

I couldn't forget the reason I was here, whether I was talking to Elijah's family, or not. And while it might be flattering to have his grandfather tell me Elijah was "taken with" me, our . . . whatever our friendship might be called at this point, was still too new for me to make light of it with his *grandfather*.

Thinking quickly, I rushed, "If you don't mind holding them for a few? I'm going to walk around and see what this fishing tournament is all about. I'll pick them up on my way out."

Was that a knowing twinkle in his eye as he accepted my credit card? "Happy to. And if you and your mom decide that you want to make fresh salmon a regular part of your menu, I hope you'll allow me the privilege of being your supplier."

"Mom handles all our menus, but I'll be sure to let her know."

After retrieving my credit card, I waved goodbye and headed down the nearest dock. I had no idea what I was even looking for. But maybe a man would jump out and hold up a sign that read "I'm a back-stabbing killer." I rolled my eyes at my stupid humor.

The first dock I chose to meander along was narrow and had several small boats attached to it. I could easily see from the end near the main hub, all the way to the other, but chose to walk the length of it anyhow. I made it to the end without seeing anything suspicious, other than two teenagers who were cozied up against the backside of a pylon that protruded through a hole in the dock. The girl wore only the flimsiest of bikinis. She had her back to the post and the boy, wearing low-slung, but thankfully much more modest bathing trunks, had leaned his arm on the pylon above her head and was speaking in a low cajoling tone. When he reached up to trace a finger along her collarbone, I cleared my throat loudly.

They jumped apart as quickly as they might have if I'd thrown a bucket of ice water on them. The girl doodled her big toe against one of the boards, seemingly very interested in the pattern her damp foot was making. The boy propped his hands on his hips and couldn't seem to stop grinning. He also couldn't seem to bring himself to meet my gaze.

I passed on without saying anything, and when I returned toward the hub, I was happy to see that the girl had donned a T-shirt, and the couple was seated a respectful distance from each other with their feet dangling in the water as they spoke.

The next dock over was lined with larger boats. It also was different from the first in that it had several side extensions. One section was filled with a tall seat and a life preserver. Presumably for quieter days, when the swimming area on the inside of this section was filled with nothing but splashing teenagers and kids. Today, there was a sign posted. "Swimming will open after the tournament."

This dock bustled with activity, and I had to swerve through the heavy crowd to avoid knocking into people. A man used a large wet broom to scrub down the side of his boat. Just past him, a couple of kids jumped up and down, pointing excitedly to some fish in the water while their mother hovered protectively behind them. Several people disembarked from a nearby boat. I paused to let them pass, then fell into step behind a couple who were jokingly placing bets on how much this year's prize catch would weigh.

I was a little irritated with their slow meandering gait, but each time I tried to pass them, someone was coming the other direction and I had to fall back in behind. Finally, they peeled off and climbed aboard a boat large enough that it had to be considered a yacht.

I was moving past a large rack filled with colorful kayaks that sat on the next outset platform, when raised voices from the boat beyond caught my attention. Just as I paused, the sun slipped out from behind the clouds above. I cupped a hand to my eyes, peered at the boat, and froze.

This boat was smaller than the yacht next door, but it was still much larger than the crafts on the first dock. But that wasn't what spiked my pulse. No. It was the item on the boat's deck—a red cooler identical to the one I had just seen in the Cookes' kitchen. At least, from this distance it looked identical. Was it only a coincidence? I mean, red coolers were a dime a dozen, right? It was probably nothing.

Still . . .

I stepped closer to the kayaks and lingered, letting the crowd slowly flow around me.

After tugging my phone from my back pocket, I pretended to scroll while I subtly peeked through the kayaks at the boat. It had a pilothouse with a red roof. And a US flag flew from the mainmast. Even though a gangplank stretched from the deck to the dock, it didn't look like anyone was on board. Nothing really looked out of place. But I'd heard those raised voices.

I moved closer and that was when I realized it was two male voices arguing quietly inside the pilothouse. Their voices drifted through a small porthole that had been left open.

The sun was coming in at the wrong angle so I could only make out silhouettes.

"Why didn't you stop him?" The larger of the two men snarled in anger.

"I'm telling you, I tried." The second voice sounded weary, like he had already explained this a dozen times.

"You must be the biggest moron in the world."

"He was stealing them!" The smaller man's hand shot out and the taller man's head snapped back.

I thrust a hand over my mouth. One of them had just punched the other!

"You cut me, you—"

I will refrain from repeating to you the string of names the injured man called the other.

"I'm just tired of you bullying me all the time, like you think you're the boss. I did what I had to do to try to stop him from stealing them."

I held my breath and leaned in closer. Had Anthony taken something despite his last words to the contrary?

The larger injured man seemed to be pressing a wad of something against his cheek now. A towel, maybe? "He didn't know he was stealing them, you idiot. He thought he had his own cooler. All you had to say was 'Hey, I think you've got our fish,' and he would have laughed and swapped you. But no. Now he's running through town with your diamonds and your knife in his back. This is no longer my problem."

My heart jumped into my throat and my phone nearly slipped out of my hands. For a moment, I was so stunned I just stood there, not quite believing what I'd just heard. Then I unlocked my phone and quickly found my video app. I hit Record.

Ducking down beside the kayaks, I strained to make out the rest of the conversation over the noise of the marina.

". . . can't wash your hands of me . . . isn't going to be happy about this . . . need to figure out what to do next." Though I could only make out part of what he was saying, the smaller man sounded desperate.

"Shelby?" A voice spoke right behind me.

With a yelp, I jumped practically out of my skin and nearly fell over.

Colleen Rice, my friend who just happened to work for Elijah at the sheriff's office, plunked her hands on her hips and peered down at me. "What are you doing skulking behind those kayaks? Elijah told me you went home. He sent me down here to cordon off the Cookes' slip."

"Shhh!" I looked around wildly, paranoid and half expecting the men inside the boat to come investigate.

Her smile fell and she hurried over to squat beside me. "What is going on?" she whispered.

I shushed her again, wanting to listen. I pointed at the pilothouse.

From inside the boat, the conversation continued. ". . . only a matter of time before . . . connect that knife back to us and then we're dead men!"

Colleen gasped.

I looked over at her, feeling certain that the shock in her eyes was reflected in my own.

My phone started ringing.

Loudly.

Hyped up as I already was, I fumbled the task of silencing it. Instead I hit the Answer icon, and then my dang thumb grazed the speaker phone button.

"Shelby? You there, hon?" Mom's voice rang clear as crystal into the suddenly much too silent marina.

All conversation from inside the boat abruptly stopped.

"What was that?" one of the men asked.

"I think someone's outside," his partner said.

My hands were numb with fear as I frantically tried to shut off the speakerphone, while at the same time keeping my attention on the porthole to see if I could catch a glimpse of a face.

"Don't just stand there! Check it out!" the larger man's voice commanded from inside the boat.

"Shel, we have to go!" Colleen grabbed wildly for my wrist, but instead knocked my phone. It slipped between my fingers, bounced once on the dock, then splashed into the water. We both watched helplessly as it drifted into the dark depths of the marina.

The cabin door banged open.

I yanked Colleen to her feet and prodded her toward the hub. "Don't look back."

We dodged through the crowd, hung a left at the main hub, and rushed for the ramp that led to the parking lot. We'd almost made it when I felt a hand clamp firmly onto my arm.

I squawked and spun, kicking out with my foot. I'm not sure if it was my recent confrontation with death, or sheer adrenaline. Maybe a little of both.

Whatever instinct caused me to do it, Elijah's grandad caught my foot right in the sternum.

"Ooof!" He tumbled backward, clutching a paper bag to his chest as he fell.

"Oh, Mac!" I scurried to help him up. "I'm so sorry."

I scanned the dock to see if any other men were rushing at us, but the area was quiet. Very quiet, in fact. Everyone nearby glowered at me. Mac was obviously a favorite around here.

"I thought you were someone else," I ended lamely. Clasping his hand, I hauled him to his feet.

He rubbed at his chest gingerly, then held out the large brown paper bag. "Just didn't want you to forget your fish."

I could feel my embarrassment in my cheeks as I accepted the bag. "Thank you. And I'm really sorry. Are you okay?"

His crooked grin was the exact same as Elijah's. Or should that be stated the other way around?

"Been a while since a woman knocked me on my . . . keister," he said. "But I'll be fine."

I still felt guilty. "I'll be sure to encourage Mom to make fish a regular part of our menu," I said as I backed up the ramp to join Colleen where she had remained.

He chuckled and retreated, hands raised. "I'm not sure this old body can handle too much more of you coming around." He punctuated the words with a wink so I'd know he was kidding, even if he did give his sternum another rub.

I opened my mouth to tease him back, but movement on the other side of the hub sealed the words in my throat.

A man, about five-ten with sandy brown hair and a puffy fishing vest, trotted onto the main part of the hub and stopped.

Across the square, his eyes met mine. His hand lifted from his side and the glint of metal in the man's hand made me gasp so much air that it actually hurt.

I was already ducking before the first shot rang out.

A Cold Steel Glower

SCREAMS ERUPTED.

The crowd scattered like alarmed cats, diving for shelter anywhere and everywhere.

Thoughts peppered through me like bullets. Bad analogy? Yeah, you're probably right. But in that moment, I instantly knew two things. The first was that Colleen and I were sitting ducks, stopped halfway up the marina ramp as we were. The second was that if anyone died here today, it was going to be all my fault. I'd once again poked my nose where it didn't belong and . . .

Another bullet sparked off the ramp near my feet.

"Colleen, run!" I pivoted and pushed Colleen up the incline.

We'd only taken a few steps when behind me, I heard a hollow *crack* and a grunt of pain.

"Stay down, punk. You're not going anywhere!"

"Mac's got him!"

"Oh! Thank God!"

Still halfway hunched against an impending gunshot, I turned to find Mac, with one knee in the shooter's back as he cinched the man's hands behind him. I couldn't make out what he was using for binding from this distance.

"Someone call the sheriff," Mac said into the silence.

It was as if the marina took a collective breath. Everything exploded into chaos.

Above the hubbub, I heard the sound of a motor.

I lifted my focus in time to see a white boat with a red roof and a US flag speeding out of the marina.

The strength left my legs and I collapsed onto the ramp. Was the man Mac had tackled the one who'd said he put the knife into Anthony's back? Maybe some good would come of this. At least we might get some answers.

No sooner had the thought registered, than I glanced back to see Elijah and his deputies surging toward us. I faced forward, and right quick.

I heard him stop beside Colleen, who was sitting just behind me. "You okay, Colleen?"

"Yes, Elijah." I could still hear the vestiges of a crush in her tone, even though she'd assured me that she harbored no hard feelings when it came to Elijah and me.

I hung my head in the hope that maybe Elijah wouldn't notice me sitting here on the ramp. It was a vain hope.

He stopped beside me, gun drawn but pointed away from me. He gave the marina a quick assessment, then holstered his gun as he looked down at me and sighed. "I'll deal with you in a minute. Don't go anywhere." With that, he moved on down to the marina, followed by his deputies.

Despite the fact that I was dreading our impending conversation, I couldn't help but admire Elijah as he moved calmly into the fray below. The crowd parted for him with respectful deference.

He walked straight to his grandfather, who still knelt by the man he had tackled and tied. Elijah hauled the shooter to his feet and handed him over to Jason, who cuffed him, then kicked his feet apart and set to carefully patting him down.

"Pops? You all right?" Elijah asked, giving his grandfather a concerned searching look.

Mac nodded. Waved a hand. "I took more of a knock from your B&B gal there, than I did from this bum."

"She's not my— Never mind." Elijah's cold steel glower skipped off me before he returned his attention to his grandfather. "What happened?"

"Red there showed up to buy some fish. While I packaged them, she took a walk. Next thing I know, she and Colleen are blitzing past me, and this fellow is trying to tag them with bullets."

Even from this distance, I could see a muscle tick in Elijah's jaw. "Of course he was. Anyone else involved?"

Mac lifted one shoulder. "Not that I saw."

"There was another man on the boat," I blurted before my brain could engage enough to tell me I should keep quiet.

Elijah faced me, hands plunked on his hips.

Oh boy, he really really wasn't happy with me this time. Had I blown it so bad that he wouldn't forgive me?

"What boat?" he demanded.

I lifted my chin. After all, I hadn't done anything that deserved getting shot at. And an uncontrollable trembling was starting deep inside. The least he could do would be to show some compassion.

I pointed toward the end of the second dock from the back. "It was tied off at the end. Just past that big yacht. But it left just a few minutes ago. As soon as Mac tackled the shooter."

"Did you get a tag number?"

I scooped my fingers into the curls tormenting my face, knowing he wasn't going to like my answer. "No. I was videoing—" There I went again blurting things I should probably keep to myself. "But, uh, my phone got knocked into the water."

Behind me, I felt Colleen touch my shoulder as she leaned to one side. "It's true. I did it. I mean, you know . . . on accident."

This time it was Undersheriff White that gave us the look that said we were quite the pair.

"All right, everyone listen up." Elijah raised his voice to be heard over the waves. "Is anyone hurt? Need medical attention?"

All around him, people shook their heads.

One man raised an arm to which he had clapped a part of his T-shirt. "Cut my arm pretty good when I was diving for cover, but I think the bleeding has mostly stopped."

I released a soft breath. Thank the Lord for small favors. With bullets flying, it was a blessing to have that as the worst of the injuries.

Elijah pointed. "Midge there will certainly have a first-aid kit on her Bayliner."

An upper middle-aged woman stepped forward. "Sure do. Come this way, George, and I'll get you patched up."

The crowd, who up until that moment had been tensely quiet and focused on Elijah, started to disperse.

"The rest of you—" Elijah thrust an arm into the air to indicate that everyone should freeze and pay attention. "Sorry. I know this isn't what you want the day before the big tournament, but I need everyone to line up to give Deputy Pyle and Undersheriff White your statements."

A collective groan rose.

"I know. Sorry. We'll try to make this as quick as possible. Your cooperation will go a long way toward making that happen."

Auggy was already setting up a makeshift table using a couple of stacks of crab-pots and a wooden pallet from Mac's fish stand.

Colleen touched my shoulder. "I better get the laptops from the cruisers. I'll be right back."

I was trembling so badly now that I could feel the metal grate of the ramp vibrating beneath me. I wrapped my arms around my knees and rested my forehead on them. How did I get myself into these situations? I was just a normal gal, honest. But ever since arriving on this island, trouble seemed to find me faster than an angry wasp could sting.

The ramp dipped and I lifted my head enough to take note of Colleen passing by to hand laptops to both Jason and Auggy. Elijah had taken over with the prisoner and was intently prodding him with questions I couldn't hear.

I lowered my forehead to my knees once more.

I needed to get Tuna to the B&B. And Mom was going to be worried sick because I hadn't been able to take her call. How much of the situation had she heard in the few seconds before my phone fell in the water?

The ramp dipped again. Elijah stopped by me, the prisoner in a firm grasp before him.

The man daggered me a glare.

There was something about his face that I should recognize, but I couldn't quite put my finger on it. If I didn't have so much adrenaline still pumping through me . . . I took a calming breath.

Elijah still had a clench on the man's arm. "He's not talking. I'm taking him to the station. I'll have to get your side of the story later. Please go home, Shelby. I'll be out later this evening."

Realization shot through me and I started to stand. "He said he stabbed Anthony. I heard him say it!"

The prisoner swore at me and his foot shot out lightning fast.

Pain exploded through my arm and I was knocked onto my backside. I scrambled backward up the ramp even as Elijah reacted.

"Hey! Knock that off!" Elijah shook the man hard, pulling back on his arms, and pushing on his calves to bring him to his knees. The man writhed and cussed. It took all of Elijah's strength to simply keep hold of him. Jason, seeing what was going on from below, barreled up the ramp to Elijah's aid.

Together, they managed to get the man into the back of the nearest cruiser. He was still kicking and thrashing so hard that the cruiser shook from side to side, but at least he was contained.

Finally able to take my eyes off the situation, I looked down. A long scrape puckered the skin along my upper arm, and by the spreading redness and swelling, I was certainly going to be bruised come morning.

Elijah was back before me, eyes wide and filled with concern. "I'm so sorry, Shelby. I should have thought. Should have kept him away from you." He reached out to gingerly take my arm. He lifted it. "This is bad. Jason, grab me a cold pack, would you?"

Jason opened the hatch of the cruiser, releasing a wave of loud cursing from the prisoner. I had a feeling if there wasn't a barrier just behind his seat, the man would have tried to make a run for it. A tremor worked through me.

"Hey. He's contained now." Elijah's soft voice drew my attention and rounded off the edges of my angst.

"Yeah. Thanks."

"How do you know it was him?"

"What?"

"How do you know he's the one who stabbed Anthony?"

"His face is clear. I saw him punch the other guy and I heard that man say 'you cut me.' Then this man said he stabbed Anthony. I think Anthony took the wrong cooler."

Jason came toward us. He massaged and shook the small plastic pillow in his hands. One of those chemical-induced cooling bags.

Elijah took it from him and ever so gently pressed it to my arm.

The cold shot a wave of pain through me, but I gritted my teeth, knowing it would soon numb the area and also would keep the swelling down.

"Uh . . . Boss?" Auggy called from the dock below.

"Be right there," Elijah called. He looked perturbed to be called away. "You'll make it to your house all right?"

"Yeah. I'll be fine."

"I need you to do something for me."

Uh-oh. "What?"

"I need you not to tell anyone what happened here until I can come and hear your first retelling of it. Can you do that for me?"

Mom was going to have such a conniption, bless her heart. I nodded. "Okay."

Elijah gave a satisfactory dip of his chin. "Good. I'll be out just as soon as I can"—he waved a sweeping gesture—"clear all this up."

Mac strode up just then, once more holding my paper bag filled with fish. "I'll walk you to your car." He stretched a hand toward the parking lot beyond the cruisers.

"Thanks, Pop." Elijah turned, and with one more glance in my direction, trotted away.

Mac helped me load the fish into Elijah's truck, then gave me a wave. "Drive safe, Red. And try to stay out of trouble, hmm?"

I smiled. "I'll do my best."

Mac hurried back toward the ramp.

Heaving a sigh of relief, I sank behind the wheel.

Tuna yowled like a banshee in a Halloween ghost house.

My head hit the driver's side glass. "Ouch! Tuna!"

As I backed from my space, I tried not to notice the cruiser that was still rocking and shaking with the fury of the prisoner inside.

I failed.

It was the sparkling hour. That time of evening when it seemed that an angel from above had swept over the Salish Sea and spilled a bowl of star bits on the water. I stood on the B&B lawn, cradling my aching arm, and simply relishing the beauty of it. With the shadowy blue mounds of the snow-capped Olympics to the east, the scene practically took my breath away.

I pulled in a long slow inhale of the salty sea air and blew it out in a slow stream. What a day.

Earlier, when I'd finally made it home and gotten Tuna inside, Mom had been near to panic and full of questions. Relieved to see me alive, she'd immediately cuddled up with Tuna, holding the cat up near her face and baby-talking to her as if I'd just presented her with her first grandchild. Tuna's purr had almost drowned out the sound of Kodi whimpering for me to pet him.

"Sure, now you purr," I'd accused as I patted the dog's soft head.

Of course, Mom had not been happy when I told her Elijah had made me promise not to talk until he came. But it had been hours now and I was beginning to wonder if he would make it tonight.

Careful to keep my injury off Mom's radar, I'd been icing my arm off and on. And had downed three Advil to help with the pain and swelling.

After Mom put her down, Tuna refused to settle. She'd paced and yowled and paced some more.

Kodi had pestered her mercilessly, dropping down till only his hind quarters were thrust into the air. He'd only wanted to play, but Tuna had immediately let him know who was boss with a hiss and one swipe of her paw.

Kodi had left her alone after that and gone to pout in his bed, just as I'd suspected he would.

Finally, after I'd helped Mom with the last of the dinner dishes, I couldn't stand the cat's restless pacing any longer and had escaped here to the yard.

I heard the sliding doors sweep open behind me. Before I even turned, I knew that it would be Elijah. I hadn't heard a vehicle, which probably meant one of his deputies had dropped him off at the end of our drive. He strode toward me, hands thrust deep into the front pockets of a pair of black jeans—these ones were disappointingly missing the rips. His hair was wet, evidence that he had just showered before coming over.

"Long day?" I asked.

"You have some idea."

I sighed and turned to study the landscape once more. I did indeed have some idea. And I wished I didn't.

He stepped up right behind me and settled his hands on my shoulders. His thumbs worked into the tight knots that strung like rope across my shoulders.

"What am I going to do with you, Shel?"

It was a rhetorical question, so I didn't bother to answer.

"If you had been shot today—" His voice broke and he made a soft sound at the back of his throat.

He dropped his hands then and stepped back and the feeling in the air was suddenly all business. "I need to take your statement."

His hardness was to be expected, I supposed. I'd known he would be super upset with me for going to the marina. How much more upset ought he be, since I'd nearly gotten a bunch of people killed—one of them, his grandfather? On the other hand, who could have known that a crazed shooter would go ballistic simply because I had been standing outside his boat?

I raised a hand. "I'm happy to give you a statement. But if you don't mind, I would like Mom to be here so that she can hear what happened along with you."

He gave me a nod and I stepped over to the sliding doors and nudged them open, calling to Mom, who was sitting at the kitchen table scrolling through her phone, to please join us.

Mom brought out sweet tea and pastries. You can take the girl out of the South but you can't take the South out of the girl.

We all sat at the wrought iron table on the cobblestone patio.

Elijah thanked Mom for the tea and then folded his hands on top of the table. His hard gaze settled on me. He set his phone in the middle of the table. "You can start by telling me what you were doing at the marina."

"I went to buy fish." The lie tasted bitter on my tongue. "Mostly."

"I asked you to go home, Shel. There was a reason for that."

Mom squirmed in her chair. "You might as well deputize her and be done with it," she groused.

"Mom, come on now." I notched my chin a little higher and met Elijah's glare. "Do you want to know what happened, or not?"

"Start at the beginning."

I took a fortifying gulp of sweet tea. "So I ordered the salmon for our dinner from your grandfather, Mac. And while he was packaging up the fish, I decided to look around the marina and see what all the hullabaloo over this tournament was about." Hullabaloo? Oh yeah, Shelby, great! Way to sound like a consummate professional. I ignored Elijah's quirked mouth and hurried on. "When I strode down that second dock, I heard two men hollering at each other inside one of the boats."

Elijah nudged his phone closer to me, and I only just then recognized that he had set it to record. "Be specific about their words, please. What exactly did they say?"

I searched my memory. "At first it was just the tone of their voices that made me stop. But then I saw a red cooler sitting on the deck of their boat. I'm almost positive that it was exactly like the one that Anthony brought to the bakery. Anyhow, one of the men inside was really upset with the other. They were in the wheelhouse of the boat. But the way the sun was shining, I couldn't see either of their faces. The first man said, 'Why didn't you stop him?' And the other man said he had tried. At that point, I think there was some name-calling. And then the second man said, 'He was stealing them!' The first man replied that he, meaning Anthony, obviously didn't know he was stealing anything. He said Anthony thought he had his own cooler. And that they should have just swapped coolers. And then he said, 'Now he's running through town with your diamonds and your knife in his back.'"

Elijah's frustrated concern was revealed by the telltale pulsing of the muscle in his jaw.

I hurried to finish my story. "The first man said something about someone who wasn't going to be happy. But I couldn't hear everything he said at that moment. Then Colleen showed up, and Mom called. Wait." I glanced at Mom. "Why were you calling anyhow?"

Mom's eyes sparkled. She lifted her phone from the tea tray, swiped the screen, and then thrust it toward me. A picture of the cutest fluffiest kitten filled the display. He was black and white with blue eyes and a pink nose. Long tufts of fur graced the tips of his ears.

"Aw. So cute!" My eyes shot wide.

Mom nodded, grinning like a little girl.

"Hold up! Did you get it?"

"Put down money. I pick her up tomorrow."

I looked back at the kitten. She was so cute that I might have to set aside my reservations about cats.

Elijah's chair legs made an impatient scraping sound against the patio. "Cute cat. What happened after Colleen showed up?"

I handed Mom back her phone and continued my story. "When my phone started ringing, the men inside the boat got all quiet. Then the first man said 'Go check it out' or something like that. Colleen tried to help me up, but we were both understandably a little nervous and flustered, and my phone got knocked into the water. We made a run for it and that man you arrested, who I can only presume was one of the two in the conversation in the boat, followed us and started shooting up the place. That's all I know." I searched Elijah's face. "Where is he now? Did he say anything more to you?"

"He's in a cell down at the station. Still refusing to talk. Has demanded a lawyer. But his lawyer is on the mainland and can't get here till morning. I figured it wouldn't hurt to give him a night to rethink his position, anyhow." His gaze skimmed to my arm. "How is your bruising?"

Mom shot straight up in her chair. "Bruising? What happened?"

Tucking my lip between my teeth, I carefully rolled up the long sleeve of my shirt. In the lights strung around the patio, a rapidly darkening purple and gold swath was clearly visible. It stretched from my elbow almost all the way to my shoulder.

Mom gasped. "Shelby Lynn! Why didn't you say anything?" She was out of her seat in a heartbeat and dashing back into the kitchen. She returned only seconds later with a large bag of frozen peas in her hand and a kitchen towel. After she had wrapped the peas in the towel, she gently pressed it against my arm.

Elijah pinched thumb and fingers to the bridge of his nose. I wasn't certain if it was frustration over my bumbling yet again into his investigation, or horror over what might have happened at the marina. "You are certain that the man who was shooting up the marina was one of the men on the boat?"

I lifted one shoulder. "I can't be one hundred percent sure, no. What I am sure of is that the boat left the marina. Right after the shooting started."

"And you're sure you didn't catch a tag number?"

Why was Elijah always asking me questions that I had not thought to get the answers to? Frustrated with myself, I only shook my head.

"And you said there might be some video on your phone? But it's at the bottom of the marina? Could the video have uploaded to the cloud?"

I winced. "I'm not much of a fan of having my phone constantly being monitored by outside sources."

Elijah gripped the back of his neck. "So that would be a no." He sighed. "I guess we'll have to send a diver for the phone and see what we might be able to pull off of it. Which means I need to get back to work." He stood wearily to his feet and pegged me with a look. But I knew what he was going to say before he even opened his mouth.

I lifted both my palms. "I know. I know. I'll be right here if you have any further questions. Thank you for your truck." I stood and dug in my pocket for his fob. "Here."

Our fingers grazed, and for a moment we stood almost toe to toe, looking into the depths of each other's eyes. His held concern and remaining hints of frustration. I hoped he could read contrition in mine. I really didn't mean to be so much trouble.

After a long moment, Elijah gave me a nod and started away. He had only taken two steps when his phone rang. He paused and pressed it to his ear. "Auggy? What's up?" He listened for a couple seconds then his shoulders stiffened. "He what?! I'll be right there."

Elijah hit the lawn at a sprint, leapt over the box hedge, and peeled rubber on his way down the drive.

Mom and I blinked at each other across the table.

Whatever that had been about could not be good. I bowed my head and said a little prayer that he would be safe.

Cat Meds and Ferry Rides

I SPENT A RESTLESS night wondering what had sent Elijah rushing back to town. My arm hurt no matter what position I was in, but that wasn't the worst part of my night.

The majority of it was interrupted with attempts to get Tuna to settle. But it was not to be. First, she paced my bed—including my pillow—like a caged tiger. I finally got up and gave her some warm milk, wondering if it would help a cat sleep like it did for humans.

It did not.

I made sure she had access to her litter, in case that was her problem.

It was not.

I noticed that enough time had passed so I could take more Advil. I downed three and tried to ignore the cat and sleep. Had just dozed off when Kodi set to yapping like his tail was on fire and I nearly fell out of bed. Tuna must have dared to approach his corner and Kodi had probably seen his little furball life flash before his eyes.

I finally kenneled Tuna, out of desperation. And low and behold, she curled into a ball, wrapped her tail around her nose, and promptly went to sleep. She must have wanted to be in her kennel the whole time.

The next morning, I woke up feeling almost worse than I had when I went to bed. I pressed my throbbing arm to my chest so it wouldn't move. I definitely needed something more for the pain. I stumbled into the kitchen and hummed with great pleasure at the smell of fresh coffee drifting on the air. There were definite perks—if you get that pun we should be best friends—to running a business with my mother. I sloshed the black brew into my mug along with a generous splash of cream, and inhaled long and deep before I took my first sip.

Ah! The nectar of the gods. Or, you know, at least a jolt of energy for bed-and-breakfast owners who were badly in need of it.

When the caffeine finally reached my brain, I took another dose of pain killers and then remembered that I had to give Tuna her meds. I went in search of Mom, who was in the dining room laying out her cinnamon roll buffet. Not gonna lie, I grabbed a plate and took two.

Mom slapped the back of my hand. "Get out of here before our guests catch you stealing their breakfast!"

"What? There's plenty." I stuffed a big gooey bite into my mouth, then covered my mouth with one hand to add, "I came to tell you I need your help. We have to give Tuna some heart meds."

Mom glanced past my shoulder and the signature smile that came out just for guests lit her face. "Good morning. I hope you all slept well?"

I turned to find the couple we'd put in the Orca room. The Alexanders, I believed. I hoped they could see my smile above my hand that still covered my mouth. "Morning, y'all. You're gonna love Mom's cinnamon rolls, trust me." With that, I hurried off before I could make an even bigger fool of myself than talking to guests with my mouth half-full. After I swallowed, I called over my shoulder. "Mom? Tuna. Heart meds. In the kitchen."

She nodded and flapped a hand to indicate I should mosey on my way. As I left I heard her hearty laugh followed by an explanation that Tuna was a friend's cat, and not an actual fish that we were medicating.

"Oh!" Mrs. Alexander joined her laughter. "That makes so much more sense!"

In the kitchen, I forked in another bite of roll and then rinsed the sticky off my hands. After that, I jogged up the stairs, let Tuna use her litter box, and then carried her to the kitchen. She snuggled and purred as she rubbed her head against my chin.

I baby talked to her and told her what a good girl she was. Maybe cats were growing on me.

As docile as the cat was being at this moment, surely Belinda must have simply been being cautious when she told me it took two people—and one wearing gloves—to give this kitty a little plunger of medicine?

Mom wasn't in the kitchen yet, so I thought I might as well try to get the task out of the way and get on with my day. I opened the refrigerator and pulled the little vial and the plunger from the cubby in the door.

The very moment that Tuna saw that vial, or maybe she caught a whiff of something, she stiffened in my arms. She let loose with a sound that was half plaintive pleading and half a growl of warning.

"Oh, come on," I said. "It's not going to be that bad. And I'll feed you right after."

Tuna was really doing her best to get out of my arms now.

"Ow!" Yikes, who knew cat claws could pierce sweatshirt material? Maybe it would have hurt less if her claws weren't digging into my bad arm. I have to say, I was in a bit of a fix trying to hold onto the meds and the cat. I plunked the bottle onto the counter and used both hands on the cat. One was necessary to extract claws from my flesh. "Ouch! Cat!"

Mom bustled in just then. She took one look at me tangoing in the middle of the kitchen with the cat and her eyes shot wide.

"Gloves!" I motioned to the kitchen drawer where we kept our hot pad mitts. "Thickest ones you can find."

Mom grabbed the pair that looked like red lobsters.

I nodded with satisfaction as she put them on. Now that Tuna and I were several paces away from the meds, she'd calmed a little. I motioned Mom forward and handed over Tuna. "You're going to have to hold her firmly. And I have to get a plunger into the back of her mouth."

"Lands almighty, Shelby Lynn. What did you get us into?" Her voice slid into a higher octave at that point. "Poor wittle kitty. What is Shelby doing to you? Is she trying to force yucky tasting medicine into your mouth? Come here, baby. It's okay."

"Just hush and hold the cat."

Mom tried, I'll give her that. But the moment I approached with what Tuna apparently assumed was liquid death, the cat went *berserk*. And I'm telling you, by her banshee wailing I'm sure the guests in the dining room thought we were slaughtering a whole passel of cats in the kitchen.

"Now, Tuna," Mom said, in the calmest tone you ever could imagine, while darting her face back from the swipe of one paw, "we don't want to hurt you."

Hiss. Yowl. Wriggle. Swipe.

Mom looked like she and the cat were in a choreographed dance.

I hadn't even gotten close to Tuna's mouth with the syringe yet.

"All right. I don't have time for this." Mom jutted her chin toward our quarters. "Get me a nice thick bath towel."

I carefully set the plunger of medicine on the counter and then darted down the hall to fetch a bath towel.

When I returned, quick as a wink, Mom had that cat wrapped up in a tight little cocoon. To my utter shock and amazement, Tuna gave one last little mewl, and then seemed to relax in Mom's arms. "There sweetheart. That's a girl," Mom cooed, rocking the cat like a cradled baby.

I may have rolled my eyes as I approached cautiously, the plunger of medicine held out of sight behind my back. Tuna glared at me, but other than that, made no fuss. I whipped the syringe from behind my back and, while Mom held Tuna's head still, I worked the meds to the back of her cheek.

She flicked her head and flapped her little cat tongue, but the deed was done.

"There you go," Mom murmured to the cat, petting her head gently. "See? That wasn't so terrible, was it? Here. Let's get you some cream. I bet that will solve all your kitty problems."

Mom gently unwrapped the cat, set her on the floor, placed a saucer on the ground, and drizzled heavy cream onto it. Tuna was purring so loudly as she rubbed against Mom's legs that I had to wonder if that towel had somehow transformed the creature before me into a different cat.

Mom gave me a satisfied smile as she handed the lobsters to me. "Best put these into the laundry. Tomorrow, I say we go straight for the towel."

I nodded, still watching the cat a bit wide-eyed as she calmly lapped cream. "I'll leave the towel by the washing machine. Thanks, Mom. You're a wonder."

She smirked. "Please. The day a cat can outsmart me will be the day I should hang everything up." Her grin stretched from ear to ear. "I can't wait to pick up my kitten."

Right. The kitten. "How much did you pay, anyhow?"

Mom hung her head a little sheepishly. "The down payment was five hundred."

"Five . . . Mom! How much is this kitten costing us?" I couldn't help but think of all the bills we had to pay to keep the B&B running smoothly.

"Now, Shelby. Don't get your pinkies in a twist. I've been—"

I couldn't withhold a hoot that interrupted her.

"What?" She eyed me like I might need to see a psychologist.

I laughed so hard that I was nearly bent double by the sink. I finally gathered myself enough to breathe out. "Mom, it's not pinkies."

"What is it then?"

"It's panties. Don't get your panties in a twist."

My dear mother's mouth fell open. Then her nose angled into the air. "Well, my version is cleaner."

I dabbed my eyes with a paper towel. "You'll get no argument from me there. But yours sounds more painful somehow. Anyway . . . how much?"

Mom held up a hand. "I've been saving. All the non-paper money that people leave on the tables. The extra change left in the rooms . . . It's all been going into the change jar in my room."

The jar she referred to was a huge five-gallon glass jug from an old water cooler. The thing was massive— taller than our knees.

"And, I've been putting in ten dollars a week for a couple of years now. So all of the down payment came out of that . . . Well, I deposited it in the bank and then paid him. The rest I'll give to him in cash today." She held up a hand. "And before you go making a comment, I'm not taking him a bunch of change. I turned the change in for cash at the bank."

"Who is this guy anyhow?"

"Someone on the Cobalt Bay Community Forums. I'm meeting him in a public place, don't worry. We're meeting in the Safeway parking lot later today." She gave a silent little happy clap.

I realized that for all her talking I still hadn't heard a price. I pegged her with a look. "Mom . . ."

She blurted, "Fifteen hundred," then winced.

"You are paying someone a thousand five hundred dollars for a *cat*?"

Mom had the grace to look a little sheepish. "She's a purebred Maine coon. When I saw her sweet face, I just couldn't help myself."

At that moment, Kodi came blasting through the kitchen with a hissing Tuna hot on his tail.

I scooped him up to save him from the feline bully. "Kodi is going to hate us."

The tension in Mom's expression eased a little. She must have been relieved that I'd dropped the subject. "Oh, he'll adjust." She headed for the sink and turned on the water. "For now I have to get back to our guests."

I nodded and left her there to wash her hands as I headed into the small laundry room just off the garage. I felt lighter somehow, and then I realized that a huge weight had just been lifted off my shoulders. After Dad died, I'd worried something fierce about Mom. She'd lost some of her verve. Become a much more solemn and quiet person. Buying this cat was the first thing she'd done since Dad left us that reminded me of the old her. I took a moment to unabashedly thank the good Lord for my crazy, impulsive, vivacious mom. After that, I took my cinnamon rolls onto the porch. I'd need to help with breakfast cleanup soon, but for now, I had a few minutes to sip coffee, enjoy the view from our back patio, and savor Mom's sweet cinnamon rolls.

I really, really wanted to go into town and find out the news. But I was determined not to make a liar out of myself this time. Elijah had made it clear that his patience with me was running short and I didn't want to ruin a good thing before it could even get started.

So after breakfast cleanup, I forced myself to do some book work and then traipsed outside to tend to the gardening.

Our hanging baskets were crazy beautiful this year. I had planted bright red geraniums in the middle, and then interspersed the edges with red and white striped petunias, lobelia, creeping Jenny, and million bells. The fertilizer that the lady down at Blooming Wonder had recommended was amazing stuff. My petunias had never been this prolific and vibrant. We'd been getting compliments on the baskets right and left.

I had just finished watering and fertilizing, when I realized I was going to have to go to the mainland to get a new phone. No way mine would have survived its plunge into the Pacific. And there was no place to purchase one out here on our little island. A ferry would leave this afternoon at two twenty. That would give me enough time to get to the phone store in Anacortes, and then catch a return ferry at six this evening.

After lunch, I did a little cleaning, and then let Mom know where I was going. She promised to keep an eye on Tuna, saying she would crate her for a little bit when she went into town to pick up the kitten. Normally, we didn't like to both be gone from the B&B, but Mom only planned to be gone for about twenty minutes, so we'd decided it would be okay this time. I patted both the cat and the dog on the head and then hurried to my car.

When I drove up to the ferry terminal, I hadn't even had time to hand over my debit card to Deb, who worked the booth, before she leaned forward, eyes sparkling with excitement.

"Did you hear the news?"

My caution raised its head. Did she mean the news about me nearly getting the entire population of the marina killed yesterday?

"I don't . . . think . . . so. What's up?" I held my breath, waiting for the axe to fall.

"You heard about the shooting, right?"

I nodded. "I was there." I thrust my card at her, mindful of the people in line behind me. "Round trip."

She accepted the card, but didn't move to swipe it. She was still leaning on the sill of the payment shack. "So you heard that Sheriff Gains arrested someone?"

"Yeah."

"Well, guess what?"

For some reason, my heart was pounding in my throat. "No idea."

She looked a little disappointed. Like she felt I could have at least tried. "The guy turned up dead!"

"What?!"

She nodded and swiped my card with great satisfaction. "Apparently, Auggy, poor soul, went to take him dinner last night and found the guy dead. But it gets worse."

"It does?"

Deb should be a news anchor. She had me hanging on her every word.

"He'd been shot!"

"Shot?!"

She nodded. Handed me back my card along with a receipt. "And Auggy never heard a sound." She leaned out the window to check the ferry lanes. "You can park in lane three behind that pickup."

I could tell by her demeanor that she was just itching to share her news with the next person in line, so I pulled ahead, thoughts spinning.

How had a prisoner been shot in the jailhouse without anyone hearing anything? Poor Elijah. I was sure that was going to be a nightmare to sort out. If I had my cellphone, I would send him a quick text to let him know I was thinking of him. But of course, I didn't.

The ferry loaded right on time, and I was directed to park in one of the outer bays where I had a great view of the water and passing islands without ever leaving my driver's seat. It was only about an hour-long crossing, so I decided to just stay in my car. I rolled my window down to catch the warm breeze and took in the passing scenery.

I knew from past crossings that islands were slipping past the ferry on both sides and that the island I could see on my side right now was called Cormorant Island.

After my restless night, I yawned big and decided it would be good to catch a quick nap in the blessed silence of my car. No pacing cats. No yapping Pomchies. I was just tipping my head back, when the sight of a boat in one of the inlets on Cormorant Island made my blood run cold.

I was out of my car in a heartbeat and gripping the rail of the ferry to take a closer look.

Sure enough. Moored to a dock on Cormorant Island, was a boat that I felt certain was the same one that had escaped the marina the day before! It had the same little red roof on the wheelhouse. The same little porthole. However, the flag flying from the mast was a Canadian flag. The boat yesterday had been sporting an American one. But that would be easy enough to change, right? This boat was too far away to read the name. I closed my eyes and tried to picture the name of the boat that had been in the Cobalt Bay marina. But it was no use. If only my footage hadn't been deep-sixed. Still all the resemblances were too close to ignore.

Elijah needed to know! I took the stairs up to the passenger deck two at a time.

Cormorant Island wasn't one where the ferry stopped. It was a private island that could only be reached by personal boat or a float plane.

I burst into the passenger area and grabbed the shoulder of the first person I saw. He was a grizzled, elderly gentleman with rheumy gray eyes. "Can I borrow your cell phone? I need to make a call. It's an emergency."

He shook his head at me. "Where's yours?"

"It got dropped in the water."

"Young lady, do yourself a favor and cut the ties. You can go a few minutes without a phone."

"No. Not today—never mind. It really is an emergency."

He waggled his fingers at me. "Move along. You'll survive."

"Please, it—"

"Next stop, Lopez Island. Next stop Lopez. Those disembarking at Lopez Island, please return to your vehicles. We will be arriving in five minutes."

Lopez Island! Oh, this was a terrible idea. A downright terrible idea. But I remembered Belinda saying that the fishing tournament started on Lopez Island this afternoon. A fishing tournament with lots of private boats. And if I got off at Lopez, I'd also be able to find a landline to call Elijah from.

I changed course and dashed down the stairs back to the car deck. I jogged to the nearest ferry worker and only felt a little guilty when thankfulness washed through me to see that he was a young man in his twenties.

I glanced the length of myself and rolled my eyes at my gardening garb. No way this was going to work. Still, I had to try. I gave my red curls a little toss and tried not to be too obvious when I lowered my lashes. "Hi, I wondered if you could help me?"

His eyes lit up, but then he skimmed me from head to toe and back again. A slight furrow settled between his brows. "Will do my best. But . . ." He grinned at me. "It will cost you."

Seriously? He was actually flirting? The guy needed better taste because I was so not looking my best. Still, I played my part. I twirled a curl around one finger, not wanting to know even the slightest inkling of what his idea of the cost might be. "I think I made a mistake back when we loaded up. I need to get off the ferry here at Lopez and I'm not sure if I'm in the right lane?"

His face pulled into a grimace of uncertainty. "Not sure If I can help you with that one. Where are you parked?"

I pointed to the outer bay. "Third car back."

He checked a list on a clipboard hanging nearby. Then looked up at me with a huge smile. "Lady, you're in luck. The two people in front of you are getting off at Lopez. So you can too. Only, you will have overpaid."

Relief surged through me as I batted the air. "Oh, that's what I get for being such a ditz, I guess. Thank you so much!"

He nodded. "My pleasure." As I started away, he called, "You wouldn't want to give me your phone number, would you?"

I faced him, walking backward up the ramp toward my car. "Oh, I'm sorry, but I don't have a phone right now. Mine got knocked into the water."

His face fell. "That's too bad."

"It really is!" I made my escape before he could realize that even if I didn't currently have a device, my number would still be good once I purchased one.

Mistaken for Homeless

IT WAS ONLY A few minutes later that I was pulling off the ferry onto Lopez Island.

Now I just had to find the marina where the tournament was starting to see if someone could give me a ride over to Cormorant Island.

But first . . . I pulled into the little mom-and-pop store just near the ferry landing and dashed inside. It was a typical small-town store with a little bit of everything from firewood to chewing gum. To my left as I entered, there were a few propane tanks and camping gear—cheap sleeping bags, a couple of tents, marshmallow roasting sticks and that sort of thing. Beyond that there were a couple rows of canned foods, boxes of crackers, and bags of chips and beef jerky. Between a couple refrigeration units filled with a variety of soft drinks, stood a stack of coolers for sale.

Huh. Those red coolers really were a dime a dozen.

To my right was the cashier's counter and a grizzled older man with white hair and pale gray eyes hunched behind it, watching me curiously.

I hurried toward him. "Hi. I know this is crazy, but I'm currently without a cellphone and I need to make an emergency call to Sheriff Elijah Gains. Would you let me use your phone?"

The man gave me an assessing look, then lifted one shoulder. "Guess that would be fine." Lifting a cane from where it leaned against the wall behind him, he pointed toward a hinged section of counter. "You'll need to come to the office, though. We don't have one out here."

"Thank you so much!" I lifted the counter and followed the tottering guy into the back. The office was stacked with extra inventory for the storefront, including plenty of camping gear and another towering stack of coolers in a variety of colors. They must sell quite a bit of paraphernalia to people who decided to do a little camping on the spur of the moment when they arrived on the gorgeous island.

We angled our way through the inventory to the far side of the room. The desk was so messy, I couldn't see the phone until the guy brushed some pages aside and motioned that I was welcome to make my call. His cane tapped out a rhythm as he went back toward the front.

The phone was one of those old mustard-brown ones with the punch-to-dial buttons on the front.

There was a wrinkly phonebook on the desk, which I was thankful for because I didn't want to call 911, since it wasn't a real emergency.

I found the number to Elijah's office and recognized Colleen's voice when she answered, "Cobalt Bay Sheriff's Office, how may I help you?"

"Colleen, it's me." I paced as far as the coiled cord on the phone—and stacks of inventory—would let me, and absentmindedly rubbed at a black scuff mark on the lid of one of the new coolers.

"Shelby?"

"Yeah, I'm over on Lopez Island." I paced back to the desk. "I need to talk to Elijah. Is he in?" The line crackled so loudly that for one horrifying moment I feared we'd been cut off.

But then Colleen responded, "Uh, yeah. One sec."

It was only a moment before Elijah's voice rang across the line. "Shelby? What's up?"

"Don't be mad." I wasn't sure what made me preface my information with that. I just didn't want him to think I was going behind his back.

"Shel . . . I don't have time for this."

"I know! I mean, I haven't done anything. I'm calling to tell you first. Aren't you proud of me?"

There was a smile in his voice when he said, "What have you got?"

"I was headed to Anacortes to get a new phone. From the ferry, I saw a boat docked on Cormorant

Island that I'm certain is the boat that fled the marina yesterday."

"Really? What makes you certain it's the boat?"

I gave him the pertinent details.

"But it has a different flag?"

"It does. But, I think the similarities are too strong to ignore. Were you able to retrieve my phone yet?"

"Jason dove for it and pulled it out late last night. Auggy has had it drying. He's working with it now to see if he can pull any of the footage you took. You said you *were* heading to Anacortes. Where are you now?"

"Lopez." I winced. He was going to chew me out for even thinking about interfering in his investigation. After a moment of silence stretched into two and then three, I dared, "If I can get someone to give me a ride over to Cormorant, do I have your permission to see if it's the same boat?"

Elijah sighed. "Do you think you can get to the Islander marina? It's on the west side of the island. I'll pick you up there in forty-five minutes."

"You will?" There was honestly nothing I could have done about the note of shock in my voice.

"Meet me at the marina, Shelby."

"Okay. See you then." I hung up. Sheesh he didn't have to sound so downright grumpy.

I reminded myself that he was all business when he was on a case. Not that I'd known him long enough to really know what he was like when he wasn't on a case, since I'd only met him a few weeks ago when poor Mabel McQueen's coffin had washed up on our B&B beach. But I just had a feeling that if I could get him away from work, he'd be a little more carefree. Not to mention that he'd been under a fair amount of stress in the past twenty-four hours, with someone he knew during his growing-up years getting stabbed to death, and then the marina getting shot to smithereens.

The owner of the mom-and-pop store gave me easy-to-follow directions to the Lopez marina. It only took me five minutes to get there, which of course left an extra forty minutes of wait time. I tipped my chair back, planning to doze lightly in case Elijah arrived sooner than he expected. All the fishermen must have left earlier because the area was quiet. I'd hear Elijah's boat when it pulled in.

Mom always said that Dad could sit down and fall asleep whenever he intended to, and I'd inherited his skill—at least when I didn't have a cat and a dog pacing and scrapping.

However, despite my intention to sleep lightly, I was sound asleep when a loud tapping on my window woke me up. I sat bolt upright and blinked hard a couple of times. I winced and rotated my arm a little. At least the pain seemed to be less severe as the day wore on. A glance at the slips through my windshield showed that Elijah's police boat was nowhere in sight.

I angled narrowed eyes at my driver-side window. Who had dared to interrupt my nap?

A uniformed deputy with a bit of a paunch and a scruffy blond beard peered in at me. "Whatever you're doing here, miss, we have a strong policy against homelessness on the islands."

My jaw gaped slightly. What about my very respectable four-door sedan said "homeless"?

He was still looking at me. "You can't sleep here, miss. I suggest you get back on the ferry and mosey on back to the mainland."

That did it. My ire was certainly in a fine feather at that point.

I punched the Start button on my car and rolled the window down. "Officer, my name is Shelby Stewart. I live over in Cobalt Bay. Sheriff Elijah Gains asked me to wait for him here at the marina. He's picking me up in a few minutes."

"Sure. And my mother is Governor Endsley's mistress."

I frowned. "What a rude thing to say about your mother! Presuming it's not true of course."

Look. I was still half asleep. And in pain because a man who had now been murdered had stomped my arm. And still more than my share of grumpy at having my nice nap interrupted. But, yeah, you're right. I should have thought my statement through a little more carefully.

Deputy Paunch, who hadn't yet given me his name, threw back his shoulders and thrust out his chin. "Listen here, you redheaded interloper, around here, we treat our officers with respect."

I lowered my face into my hands and then scrubbed my fingers against my scalp. After a moment, I looked back up at him. "Officer, I mean no disrespect. I apologize for my less than tactful response. I truly am waiting here for Sheriff Elijah Gains. I'm not homeless. Nor am I an interloper. I own and run a bed and breakfast in Cobalt Bay." I waited for him to perhaps use his mic to call in and verify my story. I could have mentioned it. But I didn't want him to feel like I was telling him what to do. I'd already gotten off on a wrong enough foot. He could at least ask for my ID and then he'd see that I lived in Cobalt Bay.

Instead, he yanked open my door. "Out."

"Excuse me?" I gaped at him. "I'm sitting here in a public place, minding my own business. I would like an explanation for why you want me to get out of my car."

Looking back, I probably should have just done as he asked. But Mom swears that every strand of my red hair has a fuse. And this man had just lit every single one of them.

The officer reached in and grabbed me by one arm—thankfully, my good one. But since I was still strapped in, his attempt to haul me out did little but cause pain.

"Ouch. Just give me a second to get my seatbelt off."

In his favor, he did release me. I pressed my seat-belt button and slowly returned it to the post. It is with a marginal amount of shame that I admit it gave me more than a little satisfaction when I stood from the vehicle and realized that I was looking down on Deputy Paunch.

I was also surprised to note how young he was. His beard was so pale that it had made him look older.

One hand resting on his gun as if I might be some hardened criminal, he motioned to the hood of the car. "Place your hands on the hood and spread your legs, please."

My jaw truly did drop this time. "I demand to know what I have done that is so suspicious."

His pale blue eyes glittered with fire. "How about resisting every command that an officer of the law gives you?"

"She's actually really good at that."

I spun toward the voice, relief sweeping through me. "Elijah! Is this one of your goons?"

"All right. That's just about enough out of you, young lady." Officer Paunch cinched one of my arms behind my back and pushed my head down onto the hood of my car.

"Hey. Hey. Hey! What in the world, Jerry? This is a friend of mine. And she was waiting here for me. What has she done?"

The metal of my hood that had been sitting in direct sun after I'd driven it here was hot against my cheek. "Not a thing but take a nap while I waited for you." I wriggled in protest and tried to stand. But Jerry Paunch was strong for being so flabby.

"She's been hostile from the moment I first spoke to her."

"He called me a homeless person. And told me I needed to get on the next ferry and mosey on back to the mainland."

"Deputy Wentz, release her." Elijah's voice was the epitome of calm authority.

Thankfully, Jerry seemed to have some respect for his boss. He stepped back, beefy arms folded, and leveled a glare at me.

I rotated my arm a few times to restore some circulation and returned his glare, pressing my fingers against my hot cheek.

Elijah took one glance at my face and tactfully stepped between us, nudging me back a couple of steps.

"Jerry, you have to have a reason to question people. Did you see open containers?"

I gasped and opened my mouth to proclaim my innocence but found Elijah's palm in my face.

"Drugs?" he continued, attention still fixed on Jerry. "Firearms in plain view?"

Jerry shuffled a little. "None of that. She was sleeping on public property."

Elijah propped his hands on his hips and appeared to be pulling in a calming breath. "There is a difference between sleeping and taking a nap." He pinned his deputy with a look. "I can vouch for Shelby, and I'll take over from here. Dismissed."

I leaned to see around Elijah. Aw, but Jerry did not like being showed up, bless his heart. His jaw swayed back and forth like an airplane homing in on a landing strip. For one long moment, he remained where he was, glaring at me.

Elijah stiffened. Took a step forward. "Dismissed, Jerry. We'll talk about this some more. For now, in case you haven't been paying attention to your radio this morning, I have some murderers to catch. And Shelby is helping me."

Jerry huffed a laugh. "I'll just bet she is."

I gasped. But Jerry was already walking away, and I clapped a hand against Elijah's arm when he took a step, obviously intending to follow.

Elijah spun to face me. Gave me a searching look. "I'm so sorry about that. What happened?"

All I could do for a moment was shake my head as I processed the past few minutes. I pressed fingers and thumb to my brow. "I came directly here after I spoke to you on the phone. I had plenty of time before you were going to arrive. I didn't sleep well last night because I was watching Tuna. And she and Kodiak had words. I decided to take a nap. Next thing I knew he—" I swept a hand toward where Jerry was just sinking behind the wheel of his cruiser. "—was knocking on my window and demanding that I exit the vehicle. I asked for a reason, and he told me that homeless people were not welcome here. I mean honestly, do I look homeless to you?" I swept a gesture to myself.

Mistake.

Elijah's mouth quirked in humor.

I took another good look at what I was wearing today. I tucked my upper lip between my teeth. Gave Elijah a bit of a glower.

He was outright laughing at me now. "You have to admit that you do have a bit of a homeless vibe going today, Shel."

I released a breath. Okay, so maybe the sweats that I had slept in last night and the sweatshirt that I had dug from the bottom of the dryer basket were not my best look ever. Plus my gardening boots had seen better days. I really needed to get a new pair. I was suddenly very aware that a man I was really interested in was standing before me and telling me I could pass for homeless. I sighed and despaired of ever making a good impression on Elijah. I really needed to up my game.

Frustration surging, I stabbed a finger past Elijah's shoulder toward his departing deputy. "That man needs to learn not to judge a working girl by the appearance of her gardening clothes!"

Elijah's chuckle could have made me even angrier, but when he said, "Don't say 'working girl,' Shelby. Just don't," I allowed his humor to raise mine.

"Yeah, probably a poor choice of words." I grinned at him wryly.

"In all seriousness, Shel, I will be taking this up with him. He was not my choice as a hire. His uncle is Hiram Wentz. He's one of the richest guys on Lopez. He insisted that his nephew be given the job."

"Well his nephew is a jerk."

"Wish I could argue with you. But I can't." Elijah, maddening grin still in place, stepped closer and tugged on one of my escaped curls. "The messy bun looks cute."

Cute. Not exactly the word a girl dreamed of hearing from the lips of the handsome man speaking to her, but at least it was on the positive end of the spectrum. A starting place.

However, I wasn't going to let Elijah get away with distracting me so easily. I clasped my hands so I couldn't follow through on the temptation to rest them on his shoulders. "Deb at the ferry terminal told me that prisoner was shot last night?"

He sighed. "Might have known word would get out about that."

I waited, but he only looked at me without adding anything further. I wrinkled my nose at him. "So that's all I get?"

One side of his mouth nudged. "What have you heard?"

"Deb said he was somehow shot in his cell and no one had heard anything."

"That about sums it up. What you may not have heard is that the window in his cell opens about four inches onto the back alley behind the jailhouse. It was hot in the cell when we put him in. So I opened the window to allow the place to cool off a little. There are also bars." He waved a hand. "No way he could have gotten out. Anyhow, based on the footage we have from inside his cell, he heard a noise, or more likely, someone called to him from the alley. He went to the window and looked out. And got shot in the head."

I slapped a hand to my mouth, face scrunching. "That's terrible!"

Elijah nodded. "Yeah. Worse, it tells me he knew information that someone didn't want to get out."

"That had to be a difficult shot, right? Like whoever took it had to have training?"

"For sure. Angled sharply upward like that? And the bullet went right through the four-inch gap, missed all the bars and took the prisoner in the head? Definitely a trained shooter. I would have said that shot was impossible."

"You had video of his jail cell. Is there surveillance of the alley?" I knew that Elijah had cameras all around the station, inside and out. "You said you think someone might have called to him? Do you know if anyone was in the back alley?"

"Yeah. We know someone was back there. And yes, there's surveillance. Unfortunately, they obviously knew about it. They were wearing a ball cap tugged low and huge sunglasses and what appears to be a potentially fake beard. They had also tampered with our surveillance camera around the corner. So we lose sight of where they go after they leave the back alley behind the sheriff's office. And that"—he lifted his palms in the air—"is the last that I can say to you about it. You do have a way of getting me talking when I shouldn't."

I pushed out my lip. "Meanie. How's Auggy handling this?"

Elijah sighed and gripped the back of his neck. "Poor guy. I mean, it could have been any of us. He just happened to be the one on the schedule to man the station that night. The prisoner was still moving when he got to his cell, but by the time he tried to stop the bleeding and was able to get a call off to the rest of us, of course whoever shot him was long gone."

"So the guy is still alive!?"

He shook his head. "Afraid not. There was nothing Auggy could do to save him. And . . ." He pinned me with a mock frown. "You got me talking again."

I lifted my palms. "I wasn't trying to, honest."

He grinned. Tipped a nod toward my car. "Do you need to get anything out of your vehicle before we go?"

"Are you really taking me with you to Cormorant Island to see the boat?"

Elijah lifted one finger and an eyebrow. "Only because Colleen is swamped at the station and due to that, you're the only one left who saw it and can potentially identify it. Got it?" He searched my face intently and, my word, could the man glower when he was trying to be imposing. "This does not mean that I give you permission to go poking your nose into things. This means that I acknowledge that you are smart. And that you are perceptive."

I liked this simmering Elijah way too much. I did not like that he sounded like he'd rather have been able to take Colleen on this trip. Jealousy didn't feel nice. Especially not when it was directed at one of my best friends.

I stepped back, reminding myself that our connection was so new that it couldn't even be called a relationship yet. And also reminding myself that Colleen had vehemently told me Elijah wasn't interested in her. I lifted a hand. "Okay."

"You're not going to make me regret this?"

I splayed my fingers against my chest. "Moi? Would I do such a thing?"

Elijah's simmer crossed the line into slight boil.

I spread both my hands, palms out. "It was a joke."

"Right then. Lock your car and let's go."

I flopped into the driver's seat and punched the power button to turn the car off. "Do you think my car is going to be okay here? Or is Deputy Paunch going to have it impounded the minute we pull away in your boat?"

Elijah sputtered a laugh, but he was too much of a nice guy to sink to my level. "I'm sure it will be fine."

I could only hope he was right.

As we walked side-by-side down to the dock and along it to where his police boat was tied at the end, the warmth of Elijah's hand spread across my lower back. I wanted to turn and look at him, but with these wide cracks between the deck boards it would be just my luck that my toe would get caught and send me sprawling. A girl's reputation could only withstand a few things, you understand. And today's thing was gardening clothes and messy buns. And near arrest.

Yesterday, well, you already know all about that. And tomorrow . . . As the Good Book says, each day has enough trouble of its own.

If Tuna Could Kill

AS ELIJAH HELPED ME up the ladder of the police boat, I was surprised to find no one else on board. I turned to face him. "Just the two of us?" My heart was suddenly beating a little faster than normal. After all, the man whose boat we were going to investigate was potentially a man who had sent one of his goons after me and shot up the Cobalt Bay marina just yesterday. And now *that* man had been brutally silenced.

Elijah stepped behind the wheel. "Everyone else was already occupied with another part of the investigation. After we—I—take a closer look, if I feel it is warranted, Jason, Auggy, and I will come back."

As he started the engine and maneuvered us out of the harbor, I took my place at the prow of the boat, leaning on the rail and enjoying the whip of the warm wind in my hair. Hooray for messy bun days. I closed my eyes and tipped my face into the warmth.

It was only a few moments before I heard Elijah give a sharp whistle. When I looked back at him he tipped a nod toward Cormorant Island just coming up on our right. I motioned for him to pull into the next channel. If I had my bearings right, the boat I had seen ought to be moored only a few slips in.

Sure enough. The boat was there, tied to a floating dock that was anchored to a cliff wall. Steps carved into the rock face of the precipice led up to a tree-lined plateau. Presumably there was a house up there, though we couldn't see any building from our level.

Elijah slowed and pulled in closer. I got a good look at the craft and gave him a nod. I was as close as I could be to one hundred percent certain it was the same boat.

Elijah angled toward the dock and cut the engine. He let our boat's momentum nudge us up against it, then tied us off. He was already strapping on a bulletproof vest. He pointed toward the hatch in the floorboards. "Get below decks, please."

I plunked my hands on my hips and glared at him. "You're really going to make me stay here?" I didn't let him see the dread crawling through me at the thought of descending into the cramped space that would be on this small boat.

"I'm really going to make you stay here. I'll be back as soon as I can." He gave another commanding nod toward the hatch.

I might have muttered a few of my thoughts as I lifted the door and squatted by the opening to the galley. In a flash, my mind took me to the back room of the mortuary and the darkness that had surrounded me as I lay on that cold metal slab. Sweat broke out on my forehead. I pulled a long, calming breath through my nose.

Elijah stopped beside me. When I glanced up, concern etched his features. "I should have thought. But I really don't want to leave you on deck alone. The galley will be safer."

"I can do this." I stood and forced my feet to move. Once I was in the room, I was fine. I wasn't on my back. There was no smell of formaldehyde. I gave Elijah a thumbs-up.

"You're a trooper. I'll be back just as soon as I can. Stay put, please?"

I nodded.

Elijah thumped the hatch closed and then the boat dipped and swayed as he presumably jumped onto the dock.

The galley was narrow and dim. But three port-holes on either side let in light. Two long benches stretched on either side of the space. And at the end a short counter held a sink, a gas two-burner, and a strapped-down coffee pot. I debated between extending my nap by stretching out on one of the benches or shoring up my energy by making a pot of coffee. I chose the coffee.

I had drunk a full mug before I felt the boat dip, and heard boots thumping on the deck above.

I suddenly had a horrible feeling. What if that wasn't Elijah up there? I hadn't been paying attention to the portholes. I should have been paying attention!

I sat on the bench, coffee cup curled in my hands, curious to know what he had found atop the cliffs, and terrified of opening the hatch in case it wasn't actually him. My heart thumped.

After only a few seconds, the hatch lifted. Elijah squatted on the deck, peering in at me.

I released a breath on a big whoosh.

"Just me. Do I smell coffee?"

"You do. Want some?"

He quickly descended the little ladder that passed as steps and sank onto the bench across from me. "You are an angel sent directly from heaven."

I smiled. "I think that would be the first time anyone has ever said that to me."

I poured him a mug and handed it to him. "What did you find?"

He gulped the coffee as though it were an elixir, and he a dying man.

"We need to get back to Cobalt Bay. The boat was empty. Nothing suspicious looking about it other than that you think it's the same one as yesterday. Up top, I took a bunch of pictures. But I want Jason and Auggy to come help me do a better sweep of the property. There's no house. Just a big cement warehouse. No windows."

"Did you see anyone up there?" I held up the coffee pot to ask him if he wanted more.

He waved me off, gulped another swallow, and set it on the bench beside him. "Not a soul. But since the boat is still here, I assume the perpetrator must be inside. I wanted some backup before going in."

"I'm glad you're careful like that."

His gaze snapped to mine. "I wish you were more careful like that."

"I'm careful."

He grunted. "You are the kind of careful that gets my marina shot to pieces."

"That's not fair!"

"Let's not fight. We need to get going." He swallowed down the rest of his coffee. "I needed that caffeine." He smiled his thanks as he stood and quickly washed his cup, then set it in the drainboard.

He headed up the ladder. I stayed to clean the coffee pot and strap it back down, but I was irritated by his barbed comment. It wasn't my fault that crazy people seemed to find me.

When I joined him on the deck once more, I gave him an exaggerated frown for good measure.

He only shook his head and gave me a look that made it clear he felt I should know he was right.

And if I was honest, I'd have to admit that since he'd known me, it was true that I'd somehow had a knack for finding trouble. I didn't suppose I could be too upset with him for his comment, especially not since he'd earlier told me he was concerned for my safety.

The boat was already exiting the channel.

Elijah yelled above the wind. "I'll take you back to your car on Lopez."

I gave him a nod and a thumbs-up.

On the way back to my car, I got to thinking about those diamonds in that fish. The man on the boat had called them diamonds, so I knew that's what they were. But all of the rocks inside that fish had been oddly uniform. They'd all been little square cubes with only slight variations. I wondered at the significance of the square diamond. Why would someone mine a bunch of diamonds and cut them all into uniform squares? Were they used for something specific in that shape?

I bemoaned the loss of my phone. If I had it right now I could be doing a little research. And drat but this little side trip had probably cost me the opportunity to get a new phone today. I stepped over by Elijah. "Do you know how late the phone store in Anacortes stays open?"

He shook his head. "No idea. But . . ." He reached into his back pocket and extracted his phone. "You can look it up. Code is three three three, seven seven."

You know, I should mention that I always try to be an honest woman, and that it was not my fault that when I tapped in the code to open Elijah's phone, the photos he had taken were all sitting in a little grid, just waiting to be viewed.

My finger had tapped the first one before I even really registered what I was doing. And by then, well, you know . . .

The cement warehouse that Elijah had talked about was a single-story building surrounded by tall evergreens. Just like he said, I didn't notice any windows. There was a large gray metal door with a keypad lock on it. And a lot of steam was coming out of a series of vents on one end of the roof.

After about the sixth or seventh picture, my guilt got the better of me. I shut down his gallery and pulled up Chrome.

As I typed in my search, I took a quick peek at Elijah over the phone.

His dimples were showing. "I wondered how many you'd look at before you shut it down."

"You were testing me?"

"Don't worry. You did a lot better than I thought you would."

I could feel heat blazing through my cheeks as I returned my attention to his phone.

My search pointed out that the Costco on the mainland was open until eight thirty. I was relieved. I was a girl made to have her phone with her nearly at all times.

If Elijah weren't so crazy busy, I would have invited him to join me for the trip to the mainland, but since he was in the middle of a murder investigation, I resisted. We said goodbye at the marina and miraculously, my car was still parked where I had left it. I'd wondered if Deputy Wentz would have it towed just to spite me.

I made my way back to the ferry terminal. The rest of my trip into town and back was uneventful. And I pulled into the driveway back at the B&B with my new phone just after ten.

Tuna and Kodi were having a fight on the tiles of the main entrance as I walked in the door. And by fight, I do mean a knock-down, drag-out, all-in fracas. Tuna was on her back, claws extended, slashing and kicking at Kodi, who leaned over her throat, yapping and snarling like she'd just shredded his last chew toy.

Two guests gaped at the scene from near the check-in desk, and dear Mom was right in the middle of the fray trying to separate the two.

I pinched the bridge of my nose. Perfect. Just perfect.

"Shelby Lynn, I may have given birth to you, but I am not opposed to taking off a limb if you don't get in here and help me."

Mom's mellow holler likely sounded to our guests like she was maintaining full control, but I knew I was about to get the short side of her temper.

I smiled at the guests, holding up one finger. "I'm terribly sorry about this. We'll be with you in just one moment. The cat's not ours. Kodiak! Stop that! Sit!"

He only laid back his ears and barked all the louder.

Tuna hissed, then howled. She swiped out one paw and caught Kodi on the nose.

He yipped and darted away from her.

I quickly snatched Tuna into my arms while Mom banished Kodi to his bed by the desk. He flopped into it, ears perked at the guests as though he'd just now noticed them.

"There," Mom proclaimed, as though all had just been set right with the world. She smoothed a hand over her hair, stepped behind the desk, and slipped on her glasses, offering a large smile to our guests. "Now, the Whites, you said?" She transferred her focus to the computer. "Yes. I see you right here. We have you in our Eagle suite. Please forgive the ruckus. Shelby will be more than happy to help you get your bags to your room." She glowered at me over her reading glasses.

Right. Message received. I'd been gone all day, leaving her to not only corral two rambunctious pets, but also see to the details of the B&B. "Of course, I'd be happy to." I eased Tuna onto the padded bench we kept in the entryway and hefted their two suitcases. "Right this way."

Sheesh. What had these people packed? Rocks?

I was in the middle of settling their suitcase on their bed and pointing out our amenities when I remembered that Mom had picked up the kitten this afternoon! Where had it been while Kodi and Tuna were scrapping? Likely hiding and terrified, poor baby. I would ask mom where it was when I got back downstairs.

However, when I returned to the entry a few minutes later, Mom was already checking in another guest. He was a single man, here on business, he said.

He and mom were so busy chatting, that Mom took his case and started up the stairs.

Since it was my turn to man the lobby, I slid the desk chair over near the computer. Tuna rubbed against my legs, and I hefted her into my lap as I opened the bookkeeping software. I was behind on some data entry work. I liked to keep up, so I never had to sit and do the dull work for too many hours at a time. I stroked a hand over Tuna's head, eliciting a loud purr. Smiling, I went to work.

I was so engrossed in the task, that I'd been there for over two hours when Kodi finally padded to my side and shook his head, making his collar tags jingle. It was his polite way of asking to go outside. "All right, buddy. One second."

I finalized the last entry, saved the file, and closed down the software. It was then that I realized Mom had never come back down. She was likely tucked away in her room already with the new kitten. Disappointment swept through me. Mom would be tired after such a long day, and I didn't want to disturb her. I'd have to see the kitten tomorrow.

I set Tuna on the floor and stood. She hissed and spat at Kodi. But he was so intent on his need for the outdoors, that he seemed to ignore the cat— thankfully! The last thing we needed was our guests leaving low reviews on Yelp complaining about fighting animals! Hopefully Kodi and the kitten would become better friends than these two.

I let Kodi out and then, when he came back in, shut down the lobby lights and locked up for the night.

I scooped Tuna into my arms again to carry her up the stairs. But even though she'd been snuggling nicely with me only a few moments earlier, this time she hissed and slapped at my hand with claws extended.

"Ow!"

She struck again.

Kodi barked at her in my defense.

"Kodi, hush!" I whispered.

Frantically, I hurried into my room and closed the door behind Kodi. He trotted to his bed and snuggled his tail over his nose.

Tuna seemed to calm the moment she saw her kennel and once I got her settled inside, I looked at the back of my hand. Long red scratches seeped blood. I sighed and went into my bathroom to wash and disinfect them.

I hoped our new kitten wouldn't be so fickle!

If I didn't know better, I'd swear Tuna could have stuck that knife in Anthony's back herself.

Square Diamonds

WITH TUNA CALMLY SNORING in her kennel, and Kodi still happily furrowed into his bed, I flopped against my pillows and tugged my laptop onto my lap.

I opened my browser and typed in "square diamonds." The first several listings were all for drool-inducing pieces of jewelry. Square rings. Cascading pendants. And even a gorgeous delicate tiara.

But then a headline caught my eye. "Our Lab-Grown Diamonds are Real Diamonds."

Lab-grown diamonds? It was an automatic click.

The article made my pulse spike as I considered the possibilities. Apparently diamonds can be grown in high-pressure chambers from tiny diamond seeds. The chamber is heated to a very high temperature and then filled with carbon-rich gasses. The carbon merges with the diamond seed. And what comes out is a diamond with the exact same chemical makeup as a mined diamond. The article even went on to say that many experts couldn't tell the difference between a real diamond and a lab-grown one.

I sat back, jaw agape, and closed my laptop. It was only a moment before I whipped my laptop open again and my fingers were flying.

Turns out there are a lot of legitimate reasons to create lab-grown diamonds. They sell for thousands, sometimes hundreds of thousands of dollars cheaper. And that makes them attractive to consumers with lower budgets. Tech companies who use them in programming chips also often purchase them in vast quantities.

So, if all of it was perfectly legal, why wouldn't the men on the boat have simply told Anthony that he had made a mistake with the coolers. If what they were doing was legal and on the up and up, they should have had nothing to hide. Of course the fact that they had the diamonds stuffed inside of fish already indicated they had something to hide.

I did a little more research. It turns out that even many large chain jewelry stores sell their own lab-grown diamonds. In 2018, the Federal Trade Commission updated its decades old rules governing language used to describe diamonds. Their new guidelines included instructions to companies that they must never use the word "diamond" to describe a lab-grown stone, unless it was immediately qualified. One company even inscribes each of their lab-grown stones with their company name so that a jeweler with a loupe can read their name inside the diamond.

My next set of searches had to do with what might happen if a company did not care to reveal that their diamonds were lab grown. After all, natural diamonds fetched significantly higher prices. So, if you could pass off lab-grown diamonds as real diamonds, you could make a huge profit.

I found a place online where a man was talking about the differences between natural diamonds and lab-grown diamonds. He stated that the carbon in natural diamonds was almost always carbon-12. Because of the way the sun interacts with carbon on the surface of the earth, it tends to be carbon-13. (Way above my head, but whatever. I was going with it.) He said, people who grow diamonds in labs tend to use whatever carbon they can lay their hands on. This is almost always a carbon-13. The article rambled on and on but finally, I got to the nugget of his post. The distinction between real and lab-grown diamonds can be determined by putting the diamond into a nuclear magnetic resonance machine to determine the ratio of C-12 to C-13.

With that last bit of information, I figured it would be hard for a company to pass off lab-grown diamonds as real diamonds for long. It might be a short-term con, but one that would definitely catch up to them.

I sighed and tipped my head against the head-board. I was nowhere closer to figuring out what might be happening with those diamonds than I had been at the start of my research.

Sleep was in order. My eyes were barely staying open at that point anyhow, after my earlier interrupted nap. I hoped for a good night, but my dreams were interspersed with mean, paunchy cops yelling in my face, dancing rough-cut square diamonds, and the handsome teasing blue eyes of the town sheriff.

I woke with a start the next morning and sat bolt upright in bed. I squinted at the clock. Six.

The doorbell rang and I realized that was what had woken me in the first place. At least with my flannel pajama pants on, it wasn't too cold to crawl out of bed at this hour. I grumbled my way into my fuzzy Pomeranian slippers and snagged a large sweater-wrap from the chair near my bed.

Who would be ringing our doorbell at six a.m.? Was it Elijah? Had something happened to him? Whoever it was, I needed to answer the door before they woke all our guests.

Six a.m.! How rude!

I yanked open the front door and froze. "H-hi." It was Garrett Cooke, and listen, I have to tell you, he was kinda cute. Elijah still had the edge on him when it came to looks, but that didn't stop me from plotting in a, you know, I'm-not-interested-but-I-should-find-someone-to-set-him-up-with kind of way. Like how had I not noticed how handsome he was the other day in the bakery?

Okay, yeah, there had been a dead body on the floor, and a sheriff I was hoping to create a relationship with nearby, so maybe I had an excuse.

"Morning." He winced. "I'm really sorry to be here so early. If ever there was a rule that allowed a son to disown his mother, it should be . . ." —he air quoted— "'If she ever sends you to the neighbor's to collect your cat at six in the morning.'"

I couldn't resist a smile. Handsome and a great sense of humor.

Colleen was still very much single with only one measly date lingering on the horizon. They would make a very cute couple. I refused to allow my thoughts to dawdle on the fact that the last date I'd thought I was on hadn't really been a date at all. That was beside the point. I needed to point Colleen in this guy's direction.

"You're here to get Tuna?" I asked. (And if there was a ringing note of relief in my voice, it was honestly not on purpose.)

"I'm really sorry. She apparently has a vet appointment with some specialist on the mainland and Mom has to catch the early ferry. She forgot in all the . . . goings-on, the other day."

I stepped back and held the door wide for him to come inside. "I'm really sorry about your friend."

He crossed the threshold with a shake of his head. "Craziest thing. I couldn't believe it when he came rushing into the bakery and just . . ." He swept a gesture. ". . . fell at our feet."

"That must have been awful."

I searched him up and down. Before I set Colleen up with him, maybe I should follow my thoughts from the other day and make sure that there really was no possible way he had somehow put that knife in his friend's back. "Had you and Anthony had any fights recently?"

"What?" He gave me a surprised look. "No. And if you're implying what I think you are, I don't appreciate it. Anthony was just fine when I walked away from the marina that day."

I raised my palms. "Sorry. It's just my nosy southern roots. I didn't mean to imply anything."

I was just apparently really bad at interrogations. But it seemed a shame to have the man closest to the victim right here and not ask him some questions.

"Do you have time for coffee? I haven't given Tuna her meds yet."

He glanced at his watch then back to me. "Coffee would be nice. But you don't need to give her the meds this morning. The vet wants to see her before she gets them today."

Now *that* was news worth waking up at six a.m. to hear.

"Great. Coffee is right this way." I motioned for him to follow as I strode to the kitchen. The hinges on the coffee cupboard squeaked loudly. I made a mental note to oil them. "We've got vanilla macadamia nut Kona, chocolate macadamia nut Kona, plain Kona, Starbucks Breakfast Roast, and several dark roasts."

At his silence, I turned to see if he was contemplating, or what. To my surprise, he was checking me out. He had the grace to blush and look down. "Uh, any of the Konas are fine."

I grabbed the nearest bag, zipped a handful of beans through the grinder, and set to scooping the heavenly scented grounds into the filter. After setting the pot to brew, I turned to face him. He'd seated himself at the breakfast bar, and this time his head was hanging as he focused on his folded hands.

"Can you tell me who the men that Anthony went to talk to were?"

He lifted me a surprised look, but then shook his head. "Police already asked me that. But no. I didn't know who they were."

"Was your friend into anything . . . shady?"

"Anything shady? Uh, not that I know of. What kind of shady do you have in mind?"

I didn't have anything concrete, so I brushed away his question and strode to the cupboard to pull down two mugs. "Do you take cream or sugar?"

"Just black, please."

"I was just wondering, you know? I mean, it seems crazy that the friends he went to greet would end up stabbing him."

"It *is* crazy. I wish I could explain it."

"Did his parents get notified?"

Garrett sighed and nodded. "Mom is meeting them in Anacortes today, in fact. They are coming back on the ferry with her to collect his body. They want to bury him in the town where they live now."

I frowned. Would Elijah be able to release the body this soon?

As if he'd read my thoughts, Garrett added, "Elijah . . . ah, Sheriff Gains. Sorry, that's still hard to say. We were on the same high school football team. Anyhow, he says he still needs a few days with the body. But they wanted to come, you know, be near him."

"I understand. Will there be a local service?" I poured coffee into one of the mugs.

Garrett shook his head in a slow way that indicated he was pondering. He gripped the back of his neck. "I think they are just planning to have a service once they get him back home."

I slid his coffee in front of him. "You know anything about diamonds?"

He lifted me a surprised look like he was wondering what on earth had brought that change of subject, which told me he at least hadn't known about the diamonds in the cooler.

"Shiny. Expensive. Women love them." He smiled softly.

"Do we ever. We're like cats. Easily pleased with shiny things." I grinned, enjoying the sound of his laugh. "Speaking of cats . . . I'll fetch Tuna."

The scrape of him turning his coffee cup on the granite countertop faded away behind me. I took a few minutes to get dressed while I let Tuna out of her crate to use the litter box. Then I crated her back up and carried her downstairs.

"Here we are."

Garrett was still at the counter, where I'd left him.

I set Tuna on the floor near his feet. "Tell your mom I'll get her litter box cleaned up and then bring it by later this afternoon along with the rest of her stuff."

"That will be fine. Listen . . ." He eyed me. "There's this diamond expo coming to Seattle next week. Would you like to go to it with me?"

It was as though a thousand watts of electricity had just shot through me. "A what?"

"A diamond expo. Companies from all over the world come to bring their diamonds. There are even booths where you can watch jewelers cut and polish a stone that you can then buy." He shrugged. "I've heard they're a lot of fun."

A diamond expo! That would neatly check some boxes for questions I hadn't had answers to until now.

Garrett's feet shuffled. "So? What do you say?"

I came back to the present. "Um . . . Listen, I hate to say no, but Elijah and I, well . . . I'm not sure what we have going, but it's not something I want to ruin before it even has a chance to get off the ground, you know? I'm really very flattered, but I have to decline."

"Ah. He beat me to it, huh?"

I wanted to tell him he was still behind the starting line, despite being pretty cute. But all I said was,

"Yes. But I have a friend named Colleen. Would you consider going on a double date?"

"Colleen Rice?"

"She's the one."

A measure of caution seemed to fill his features. "We actually dated in high school."

I tried not to chafe too much at the way he'd so quickly recovered from my rejection.

He continued, "If you can talk her into spending a day with me, I'll eat my socks."

"Tasty," I teased.

"Yeah." He grinned. "She's not my biggest fan. In addition to that, she's much too smart for me."

"Oh, come on now, don't sell yourself short. I won't make any promises on her behalf, but I'll ask her and see what she says and get back to you."

He hefted Tuna's crate. "Sounds good. Thanks."

After I saw him to the door, I closed it and pressed my back to it. My heart was beating at least nine hundred beats per minute. This could be a huge break in the case. I needed to call Elijah and tell him about it and confess that I may have committed us to a double date—providing Colleen wanted to go on a date with Garrett.

I was reaching for my phone, when I remembered the hour.

Drat. I'd have to wait at least two hours until his office opened.

The Kitten Scammer

I WAS ON MY way up the stairs with my coffee when I met Mom coming down. She dashed at her cheeks when she saw me approaching. Wait. Was she crying?

"Hi Shelby Belle. What are you doing up this early?"

"You didn't hear the doorbell?"

She was definitely avoiding looking at me. "The doorbell rang? It must have been when I was in the shower. Who was it?"

"Garrett Cooke. He was here to get Tuna. Mom? Have you been crying?"

Her face crumpled. "Oh Shel Belle, I just don't know what to do."

My heart thumped. Things must be dire for real, because she only pulled out my old nickname when she was feeling really emotional.

I took her arm. "Come on. Back to the kitchen. I have coffee and I'll get you one of yesterday's cinnamon rolls." If that undersheriff, Jason White, had hurt my mother, he was going to get the sharp side of my tongue!

Mom sank down at the kitchen island and after I'd put coffee and sugar-laden baked goods in front of her, I sat on the stool beside her.

"What is it."

Mom forked in a sticky bite of cinnamon roll, and washed it down with coffee. "I'm so stupid."

"You are not! You are the smartest woman I know. And if that idiot man has made you feel like this, well, he can kiss the bottom of my shoes!"

Mom blinked and gave me a surprised look. "What idiot man?"

"Undersheriff White!"

"Oh." She batted her fork through the air. "This has nothing to do with Jason."

"It doesn't?"

Mom dropped her fork and propped her head on one hand. "I got ripped off." Tears burgeoned in her eyes again. "I'm just so mad and disappointed and . . . stupid!"

"Mom! Stop that. What happened?"

"I went to get the kitten . . ." Her tears overflowed.

"Oh yeah! The kitten." A rock dropped into my stomach. I should have remembered to ask about the kitten the first moment I'd seen her this morning. Maybe it was good that I hadn't had a chance to ask about it last night. "What happened?"

"I showed up at our set meeting place and the man wasn't there. And guess what? Marnie was there too!

She put a down payment on one also and was going to give it to Jordan for his birthday because he's been wanting a Maine coon. But . . ."

"Was he just late? How long did you two wait?"

"We waited for over an hour!"

"Maybe something just came up? Can we call him?"

Mom swiped more tears. "I tried. The number from the ad now just goes to an automated message that says the number is no longer in use."

I felt my jaw go slack. "The cute kittens were a rip off?"

Mom only slumped further over her coffee cup.

Five hundred dollars. Ugh. With the way things were going, after our expenses with the B&B—mortgage, food, and insurance—that was about all we profited each week. But we loved our work and we had food and a place to live that was breathtakingly gorgeous, so it had never seemed like a real hardship. But if anything extra cropped up like a trip to the vet, or a health issue, we were going to be in a tight spot and right quick. It had been lingering at the back of my mind, I knew. And knowing Mom, I'm sure in hers too.

I slung an arm around Mom's shoulders and propped my head against hers. "It could have happened to anyone. I'm kinda bummed we aren't going to get that kitten, though."

Mom dashed more tears with a little laugh. "Me too."

"Wait! How did you pay him? Because we could maybe file a fraud alert and get it back!"

Mom sniffled and mumbled, "Cash."

I straightened and looked at her. "You sent five hundred dollars cash to a stranger selling kittens on the internet?" Too late, I realized that my tone seemed more than a little condescending.

"I told you! I'm so stupid!"

"No, Mom, no. I'm sorry. That came out wrong. Did Marnie send him cash too?"

Mom nodded.

"What's the address?"

A wimpy flip of Mom's hand seemed to banish my idea before I'd even stated it. "I already thought of that. But it was to a PO box in town. The lady at the post office said she's not allowed to give me any information about who rents it."

"She might not be allowed to talk to us, but she certainly would have to talk to law enforcement." I straightened and downed the last of my coffee. I gave Mom one last side hug. "Buck up, Mom and finish your roll. I'm heading into town."

"Be careful, Shelby."

Oh good, we were back to Shelby. That meant she was feeling more like herself. "I will. I'm just going to talk to a certain someone who can maybe help us."

"Tell Elijah I say hello."

I only smiled. Let her think I'd meant Elijah, but I couldn't bother him with this. He was embroiled in a couple of murder investigations. No. This problem needed to be laid on the desk of someone else. Someone who cared about my mother. And I knew just who.

By the time I put on some makeup and made it into town, there were still fifteen minutes before the police station opened. I tipped my head against my headrest, relishing the warmth of the sun. I spent the time talking to Jesus and reminding Him that our little corner of the world existed and that we needed His help with a few things. I knew in my head that He hadn't forgotten us, but sometimes the heart needs reminding, and talking to Him sure does that for me.

By the time Colleen arrived and unlocked the station door, I was feeling quite a bit lighter.

I slipped out of my car and poked my head into the police station. It was small. From the front door, I could see all the way to the back offices, and even catch a glimpse of the hallway that led farther into the building, where I'd been told the cells were. All the cells here were temporary holding cells. No one ever spent more than a waiting period here. Sleeping off a drunk. That kind of thing. The building was built on a slope, as most places were in our little town. And the cells were on the tallest side of the building. High enough that they had the small windows Elijah had mentioned—I'd seen them from the outside—but high enough that they should have precluded anyone being able to aim through them to shoot a prisoner.

I wondered if Elijah had any leads on that front yet. Speaking of that man . . .

He was walking toward me from his office, and he actually looked a little pleased to see me. "Morning," he offered.

"Good morning. I hope you found some time to get a little sleep last night?"

He held finger and thumb a spare inch apart. "What can I do for you?" His gaze flickered over me, and I was glad I'd taken time to do my hair and put on a little makeup this morning—a girl had to do what she could to overcome past impressions—especially when she'd been told she looked homeless. "I'm actually here to see, Jason . . . uh, Undersheriff White. But after that . . . Do you have five minutes? Garrett Cooke came to talk to me and I have some things to tell you."

"Sure." He led me toward the offices and paused by Jason's door. He peered around the doorpost, leaving me ample room to pass him. "Jason? Shelby Stewart is here to see you."

Jason looked up from his monitor and gave me a warm smile, even if there was a bit of surprise in his eyes. "Morning, Shelby. How can I help you?" He rose and motioned for me to enter.

I paused in the doorway and said to Elijah, "This shouldn't take long."

He tipped a nod down the hall. "Meet me when you're finished and we can talk."

With that, he strolled on down the hall to his office which was the next door down. I leaned back. I couldn't help but enjoy the sight of him fully decked out in that tan uniform this morning. Ooh la la, the man wore that uniform well.

Undersheriff White cleared his throat pointedly.

Feeling warmth in my face, I hurried into his office. "Mom needs your help."

Concern immediately filled his expression. "She does?" He stood and reached for the coat on the rack behind his desk.

I raised a hand. "Not this minute. She's fine. It's just that she got ripped off." I filled him in on as many of the details as I knew, including the fact that Marnie had apparently been a victim too. "So, I was wondering if you might have any pull with the post office? Can you get the name of the guy?"

He nodded. "It can take some time. But I'll look into it, yes. And thank you for coming to me. I'll call your mom for further details."

"Thank you." I studied him for a moment, trying to decide what it might be like to have him as a stepfather. Obviously, he and Mom had made no strides in a relationship, other than to be on friendly terms. But he was a handsome widower and Mom was a beautiful widow. They connected. They liked each other. I had a feeling that it was going to turn into more someday soon if they didn't get in each other's way, and while it panged my heart to think of Mom moving on without Dad, it also filled me with joy for her. The idea was growing on me. Maybe they needed a little prodding in the right direction.

Jason shifted in his chair. "Anything else I can do for you?"

I leapt up. "Nope. Thank you for looking into that for us." I hurried toward the door before I could do something silly like—I stopped, and turned back to him. "Would you like to come to dinner on Sunday after church? Well, more like lunch really, not dinner, but it's a Sunday so maybe dinner is the right word . . ."

I bit my lip to silence my nervous chatter. Mom was going to kill me.

Officer White narrowed his eyes at me. "Did your mother ask you to ask me?"

"No. She wouldn't do that. But she also wouldn't mind me asking you to join us." Lies. "Just a friendly lunch. Nothing more. We're . . . trying to get to know people in town better."

His contemplative gaze made me squirm.

Finally, he said, "Okay. Thank you. I can follow you home after service."

"That would be perfect." I made my escape before he could change his mind.

Down the hall, Elijah had left open the door to his office. When I tapped on the doorframe, he stood and strode my way as he motioned me to a seat.

After he closed the door, instead of returning behind his desk as I'd expected him to, he sat in the chair next to me. "Garrett, huh?" His gaze searched mine.

Was that a little jealousy, I detected? I have to admit that it did my heart good.

"Tuna had a veterinary appointment. He came by to collect her early this morning."

"And you talked."

"We did. And . . ." I winced. "I might have invited him to go on a double date with me, and you, and Colleen."

He sat straight upright. "Me and Colleen?" He was already shaking his head.

"No." I shot out a hand. "I listed the order wrong." I swung a finger between us. "You and me, and Garrett and Colleen."

He relaxed a little, scrubbing one hand over his jaw. "I see. And where are we going on this double date?"

I felt quite pleased with myself about this one. I rested my hands on my bag and fiddled with the handles. "To a diamond expo." I watched his face closely and was not displeased.

He angled more toward me, giving me a searching look. "A diamond expo? Where is this at?"

"In Seattle. It starts on Thursday and is supposed to go all week. Diamond collectors and buyers are supposed to be there in droves. And it's open to the public, too."

Elijah roughed his fingers through his hair. I could almost see the cogs whirring inside his head.

After a moment, he pinched the bridge of his nose and closed his eyes. "I should have checked on things like that."

"You should have checked to see if there was a diamond expo? Come on, E. Don't be so hard on yourself. You've been a little busy with a couple murders. Did you ever figure out how the guy in your cell got shot? What was his name, anyhow?"

"Kevin Swift." He sighed, shoulders falling. "And no. No new leads on that front. It just grates on me to know that guy is out there walking around."

I shivered and wrapped my arms around myself. It didn't exactly give me great comfort to know that I was living on an island with a murderer on the loose.

"Hey." Elijah reached over and settled a hand on my shoulder. "We're doing everything we can to catch these guys. I promise you that." He glanced at his watch. "I hate to break this up, but I have to go. Jason and I are heading back to Cormorant today to check out that warehouse."

"Be careful, huh."

"Yeah, I will. And if you can talk Colleen into going on a date with Garrett, I'm in. I'll take this as a yes to my request that you let me take you on a date just before we got the call about Anthony's murder?"

I clasped my hands beneath my chin. "I will forever regret that I wanted to savor that moment and was slow to respond. My answer would definitely have been yes."

"Good." He gave me a wink, then stood and stepped from his office, holding the door for me to follow. "This way, you'll be close when the trouble starts."

There was something in his tone that raised my hackles. "What do you mean by that?"

He turned and faced me, walking backwards for a few steps. Finally, he grinned and spun forward, offering me nothing more than a little wave over his shoulder. "Gotta run, Shel. Just talk to her."

I could see Jason waiting for him near the front doors. I hoped Jason would have time to look into Mom's situation soon. But obviously, tracking down a murderer would need to come first.

My focus swung back to Elijah as the two men stepped outside. I folded my arms with a huff. *When the trouble starts?* He obviously thought I was going to cause some sort of havoc at the diamond expo!

"Just talk to who?" The very woman of our conversation appeared by my side.

I looked at her, releasing my pique with Elijah as I felt an incomprehensible dread rise inside me. I had the impression that Colleen wasn't going to be thrilled with our plan. "You."

"Me? About what?" She motioned for me to follow her to her desk.

"How are things going with Mason, the writer? I haven't heard you talk about him in a while."

She waved a hand over her shoulder as she meandered through the officers' desks. "He hated living on the island and moved back to Kentucky."

"Bummer. Were you heartbroken?"

She couldn't be too heartbroken, since she hadn't even mentioned his parting to me.

She paused by the watercooler and thrust a cup under the spout. She tilted her head in thought for a moment. "Not really, I guess. He was nice and all, but then he sort of started getting clingy. He was pretty upset when I told him I didn't want to move back to Kentucky. I was actually kind of relieved when he left. Now stop dodging my question. What did you need to talk to me about?" She started toward her desk again.

"Garrett Cooke."

She froze, then spun to face me so fast that I nearly got soaked by the water that sloshed out of her cup. One of her hands plunked onto her hip. Her frown was immediate and deep.

"That rat? Why do you need to talk to me about him?"

I tucked my lip between my teeth. "Rat, huh? I thought he was kind of cute."

Colleen waved her half-full cup of water and resumed her trek toward her desk, only this time she looked like she was trying to punch holes through the floor with every step. "Oh, he's kind of cute all right. Gorgeous, even. He's also a jerk . . . know-it-all . . . jock . . . major pain in my . . . Well, you get the picture."

I sat in the chair across from her desk. "So a double date with him and you, and Elijah and me is out of the question?"

Colleen swung her hand like she was chopping someone's head off. "Out of the question."

"It's to a diamond expo."

She stilled, peering over at me, interest clearly piqued. "A diamond expo?"

I nodded. "And I'll even get Garrett to promise to buy you a diamond. He can afford it. Belinda mentioned once that he's made millions in real estate."

"Of course he has. He was always a go-getter. But—" She laughed. "The last thing I want from Garrett Cooke is a diamond! The very, utterly last thing."

"So you'll go? It's part of the investigation."

Colleen sighed and glowered at me. "You have no idea what you are asking of me."

I waited patiently.

Finally, she tossed up one hand. "Fine. I'll go. Dang, Shelby, you could talk a turtle into giving up its shell."

The Diamond Expo

ON THE MORNING OF the diamond expo, we all piled into Garrett's gorgeous bright-yellow Mustang and headed for the ferry terminal. Poor Elijah, who was sitting next to me, practically had his knees crammed into the back of Colleen's seat. She hadn't seemed to notice, and I didn't want to embarrass her in front of everyone in the car by pointing out that she could scoot her chair forward. There seemed to be a sizzling wall of hostility surrounding Colleen. She had her arms folded, and from the side of her face that I could see, was glowering out her window with enough force to make all the animals in the forest cower.

Elijah didn't seem any more intent on making conversation than Colleen, though his stance and attitude seemed neutral. He was simply deep in thought, probably pondering his case. Since Garrett was quietly concentrating on his driving, I figured that left it up to me to break the tension in the car and make conversation.

"I really like your car, Garrett," I said as I ran a hand over the buttery black leather of the back seat. "How long have you had this?"

He met my gaze in the rearview mirror and gave me a wink and a nod of thanks. "I just got this one a couple of months ago."

"What year is it?"

"Brand new. This year's release."

For some reason, his words caused Colleen to grumble something under her breath and squirm around in her seat. I wasn't sure what that was about, but I didn't have to wait long to find out.

As Garrett maneuvered into the line at the ferry terminal, Colleen angled so that her back was pressed to her passenger door. Arms still folded, and glower still firmly in place, she gave Garrett a scathing once-over. "So glad to see that all of your dreams have come true."

Garrett's shoulders seemed to sag a little. "Not all my dreams came true. And you know that very well. If you'll recall, I asked you to come with me."

Colleen flounced around to face forward. "Oh, I recall it with vivid clarity."

Brows raised, I glanced over at Elijah. Their little tiff had even snapped him out of his thoughtfulness. He gave me a subtle shake of his head that said I should not pry.

Okay. So I should change the subject. "What do you do for work, Garrett?"

Colleen growled audibly and angled toward her window, presenting Garrett with the back of one shoulder.

Garrett pulled up to the ferry terminal's payment booth and handed Deb his card. Then he met my gaze in the rearview mirror again. There was a little sadness in his eyes this time. "I am in the marketing and sales department of a retirement home on the waterfront in Seattle. And I dabble in real estate."

Dabble? So that was what millionaires were calling it these days. I only knew his financial situation because of things Belinda had told me.

Garrett accepted his card back from Deb at the booth and pulled us into the lane she directed him to.

Colleen was so angry now that I could see a muscle twitching in her jaw.

I really wanted to ease her tension, but every line of conversation I tried to start seemed to only agitate her more. Why was she so upset about him working in a retirement home? That seemed like a respectable line of work to me. I made a mental note to ask her about it later. For now, I decided that the better part of valor might be for me to just hold my silence like everyone else in the car.

We drove onto the ferry, and when Garrett parked, no one moved.

Okay, I guessed we were all remaining in the car for the crossing. I would have liked to go up and have a bowl of the Ivars clam chowder that they served on these ferries because it was the best I had ever eaten, but I didn't want to cause any more angst for my friend. So I grudgingly remained where I sat. My stomach rumbled in protest.

Elijah glanced over at me with a grin quirking up one side of his mouth. "Hungry?"

Relieved, I nodded.

He tipped his head toward the stairwell out his window. "They have food in the galley. Want to go get something?"

I nodded like he had just offered me the world.

He chuckled and opened his door and I scrambled after him.

Once we reached the main deck of the ferry, I blew an exaggerated sigh of relief. "Wow. Talk about tension that you could cut with a knife."

Elijah nodded. "They have history."

"Really? I never would have known!"

He chuckled. "Sarcasm noted. Sounded like you are as hungry as I am?"

I nudged him toward the galley. "I'm starving. And I love clam chowder. I never knew what I was missing until we moved to the Pacific Northwest."

"Good. My treat."

As we walked the length of the passenger deck toward the restaurant, almost everyone gave Elijah a nod and a word of greeting. He took time to stop and say hello to each one who greeted him and while

I appreciated his kindness and concern for his constituents, I despaired of ever getting my soup. But when we finally made it to the galley, the line in front of us was short, so that was a bonus. The self-serve restaurant was a U-shaped section in the middle of the ferry deck, with choices of foods lining the edges. We each took a tray that slid along a set of metal tracks and began loading them with food.

I ladled chowder into the largest-sized container and added a chocolate muffin to my tray. Elijah chose the chowder and a salad.

I wrinkled my nose at his healthy choices.

To which he responded with a pointed finger. "One of these days, you are going to regret your lack of vegetable intake."

I only laughed and popped a piece of my chocolate muffin into my mouth.

Elijah rolled his eyes and handed his card to the cashier.

I bumped him with my shoulder. "Thanks for paying."

He looked down at me, and sweet mercy, but I would never get tired of looking into this man's eyes.

"My pleasure."

His gaze roamed my features for a second but then the cashier cleared her throat. She was holding out his card with one brow lifted.

Elijah gave her a sheepish smile and took his card. "Thanks."

We lingered over our chowder until the pilot announced over the speakers that everyone needed to return to their vehicles, and then we made our way back down to the vehicle deck. When we climbed into the back seat, I couldn't tell whether there was more or less tension in the car. I glanced between the two in the front.

Colleen seemed to be less frowny, but Garrett seemed to have slumped further into in his seat.

I decided to let the silence reign this time.

I focused on the scenery out my window. The ferry docked and we followed our lane off the boat and out of the terminal. Washington was probably the most beautiful state I had ever lived in. Almost everywhere I looked on this gorgeous clear sunny day, I could see one snowy mountain or another. With evergreen trees lining the highway, and farm fields interspersed along our route, shades of green surrounded us. Even the large cement blocks that shored up the sides of the freeway in places had decor on them. Some had a variety of leaves stamped into the blocks. We passed another engraved with a scene of swimming Orcas.

Though we had lived here for several months, I hadn't yet traveled to Seattle. And when the freeway crested a high overpass and downtown Seattle came into view, I pulled in a breath of awe. The Space Needle was off to one side of a section of towering skyscrapers. And in the foreground, sunlight glinted of the most beautiful blue water.

"That's beautiful! What body of water is that? The Pacific?"

Beside me, Elijah bent to get a better look out his window. "No. That's Lake Union. It's freshwater, but actually connects the Sound to Lake Washington."

"Gorgeous! What an amazing view."

Elijah nodded. "Yeah. It really is. Especially on days like today."

I sat back with a satisfied sigh, making a mental note that I wanted time to explore Seattle in more depth one of these days.

Garrett exited the freeway and headed into the heart of the city. I would've been lost inside five seconds with all of the one-way signs and blocked-off intersections, but Garrett seemed to know the streets like the back of his hand. We made so many turns that I was all confuzzled by the time we arrived at the expo. But the moment we parked and climbed out of the car my awe was once again in full force.

The building adjacent to the parking lot was huge. Like airplane-hangar-times-ten huge. It stretched for probably three blocks and had long windows at the top near the roof. It looked to be at least three stories high, but through the massive sliding doors that were currently being pushed open by two security guards I could see that the interior of the building was all one story.

Elijah stopped beside me and, with a chuckle, gave my chin a gentle bump with his finger. "Don't want you catching any flies with that hanging open like it is."

I laughed. "Doesn't it just amaze you that we can build something like this?" I stretched my arms to indicate the vastness of the building.

"Yeah. I guess it is pretty amazing." He prodded me forward with a hand to my back. "We better catch up with Garrett and Colleen."

I hurried, almost having to trot to keep up, mostly because my attention kept wandering. We darted around many other people who were apparently also here for the diamond expo, and joined the long line outside the doors. "Wow. Looks like we're going to be here for a while." I was certainly glad that Elijah and I had taken time to eat on the ferry.

Garrett and Colleen remained in their own silent bubbles.

But Elijah offered, "You'll be surprised at how fast the line moves when they start to let us all in, which should be . . ." He consulted the time on his phone. "In just a couple minutes."

He was right. We didn't have to stand around for long. And as soon as the guards motioned that we could enter, the line surged ahead as though we were all escaping a tsunami.

And let me tell you, if I thought the vastness of the building was awe-inspiring, the sheer amount of glitter and glam inside had me catching my breath. We ambled past table after table laden with diamond necklaces, and bracelets, and tiaras, and rings. There was even a booth that specialized in collars for pets.

Elijah bumped me with his elbow. "Want to get Kodiak a diamond-studded collar?"

I laughed. "That little yappy furball certainly doesn't get a diamond collar before I get something."

Ahead of us, I was happy to see that Garrett and Colleen were at least speaking to each other. I even saw Garrett smile at one point, though I had not seen a smile from Colleen yet.

It was about at that point that I remembered we were actually here to see if we could find any clues about the square diamonds inside the fish. I leaned close to Elijah. "So do you think in all of this that we're ever going to be able to find any clues about those diamonds?"

He lifted his gaze and scanned the building. Shook his head. "Seems like hunting for a needle in the proverbial haystack, doesn't it?"

He was right. The building was so large that with the crowds of people, we couldn't even see all the way to the other end.

I looked at Elijah with a wicked grin. "I guess we are just going to have to visit every single booth."

He laughed. "I'm sure that will be torture for you."

I liked that we got each other's wit. "Oh, for sure!"

He held out a hand and motioned for me to proceed to the next booth. I scanned the display of rings, not really impressed with all the bands encrusted with tiny diamonds. And we moved on.

But the next booth was fascinating. And not only was it fascinating, but it got my heart rate pumping. Because as we approached there was a man hawking the benefits of their booth.

"You look like a lady who would enjoy a custom-made diamond ring, am I right? Step right here under our awning and your man can reward you with your own custom jewelry."

I felt my cheeks flame at his assumption that Elijah was "my man."

But he was still talking and didn't seem to notice my discomfort. "You can even watch Ted there, cut and polish your stone. Our prices are low. And I guarantee you won't find a better deal anywhere in the building. Especially not for a custom piece."

The man named Ted was at that moment presenting the woman ahead of us with the ring she had apparently ordered. He handed it to her with a slight bow and clasped his hands behind his back, waiting for her feedback.

She slipped it on her finger and held her hand out at arm's length. "Oh my! It's perfect!"

Ted beamed. "Wonderful. Enjoy your day."

As the woman came toward us, her excitement overflowed. She held out the ring for me to see. "Isn't it gorgeous? It's from a real diamond mine in South Africa but only cost fifteen hundred dollars! Isn't that amazing?"

I took her hand and admired the large stone on her finger. It was an oval cut surrounded by several smaller ones.

"Beautiful!" I said. "How do you know for certain that it is a stone from South Africa?"

The woman blinked a couple of times and then sputtered in confusion. "Well . . . I guess . . . I just believed what they said."

I met Elijah's gaze for a moment and then returned my focus to the woman and gave her a smile. "Well, it's beautiful."

"Yes. Thank you."

Elijah nudged me to hurry forward until we caught up with Colleen and Garrett. He prodded us all to the edge of the building, where we had a little more space.

"Guys, I have an idea." Elijah's gaze landed on me as Colleen and Garrett leaned in closer. "You're not gonna like it."

I felt my brows nudge into my hairline. "Intriguing."

Elijah smirked. "What do you say to marrying me?"

"Wh-what?"

He was grinning outright now. "Only pretending, of course. Garrett, you and Colleen can do the same. Colleen, obviously you know we are hoping to find someone with a cut on his face. But if you see anyone who looks familiar from the marina, give me a call. Each of us is here to find an engagement ring." He air quoted "engagement ring."

Poor Garrett shuffled his feet like a sixth grader with his first crush as he eyed Colleen. He hung his head, gripped the back of his neck. "As long as it's all right with Colleen."

I have to give Colleen credit for the fact that she seemed to realize it was the only way we were going to make any progress in a room of this size. "Fine." She rolled her eyes. "Let's get it over with."

The grimace that stretched Garrett's face tugged at my heart. Colleen seemed set on being hard on him today.

"All right then," he said.

Elijah gave a nod. "Thanks, guys. You two take that aisle and Shelby and I will take this one. Remember, whatever scheme these guys are involved in, they've already proven that they're willing to kill for it. So be careful and be on your guard."

Garrett returned his nod. "Don't worry. I'll keep her safe."

Colleen huffed.

I couldn't help but smile as he and Colleen walked off. It would be a miracle if they convinced anyone that they were here to shop for an engagement ring.

"Think they can make it through the day without killing each other?"

"They'll be fine." The tug of Elijah's hand urged me forward. "Ready?" he asked.

I grinned up at him with a bat of my eyelashes. "Whatever you say, darling." Even though I had only been kidding, I felt immediate heat blast through my face.

One corner of his mouth quirked up. "Right. To work then."

I swallowed as I took in the grandness of the displays in the building. How were we ever going to find one crazy diamond . . . smuggler? Dealer? We weren't even quite sure what we were looking for.

"One booth at a time, like you said."

I glanced up at him, wondering at his ability to read my mind.

"Here we go. You ask about engagement rings. And while you're doing that, I'll check out the rest of the inventory."

"Sounds good." We had a plan. I like having a plan.

I approached the woman at the first booth on our right. Beamed at her. "Hi there! We are in the market for an engagement ring. Just wondered what you could recommend to me?"

The woman's face lit up. "Oh, hon! Have we got the perfect rings for you!"

She pulled a little drawer from the base of the display stand and set it before me with the sweep of her hand. The drawer held a deep-blue, velvet-lined tray with ring after ring cushioned in wide rows. I tugged free the first one that caught my fancy and almost choked when I saw the price tag.

"Do you know what size your finger is?" she asked.

I swallowed and held out my ring finger. Beside me, Elijah chuckled and touched my right hand to lower it to my side. He reached across me and lifted my left hand, grinning down at me. "Let's get the size on the correct finger."

I was embarrassed. Of course an engagement ring needed to go on my left hand. What a silly blunder. But Elijah had simply smoothed the moment over.

He looked at the woman behind the booth. "You're our first stop. So if you could measure her finger, that would be great."

"Of course." She chuckled. "It's quite normal for a newly engaged woman to be nervous. Don't feel bad."

Elijah moseyed off to look at the diamonds at the other end of the booth. I also caught him checking out what was behind the booth, and even, when the woman bent down to retrieve something, lifting the skirt of the tablecloth to get a quick peek under her table. He was beside me again before the woman could set a little hinged wooden box in front of me. The box had a variety of sizes of wooden posts, each holding a single plain silver ring.

"Now then . . . looking at your finger . . . I think you might be close to a . . ." She tugged one of the rings off of a smaller post and thrust it toward me. "Size five?"

I took the band and slipped it onto my left ring finger. She was right on the money. The band fit me snugly but still had a little room to spare.

Elijah settled one hand at my back. "Size five it is, then. But I don't want us to buy a ring at the first booth we've stopped at. These are lovely though." He smiled at the woman. "Thank you for your help."

She nodded. "Not a problem." She held out a business card to us. "If we can ever help you with anything, just give us a call."

We took the card and moved on to the next booth. And that was pretty much how the entire morning went. From booth to booth, we gathered business card after business card and not a single clue. No one seemed suspicious. Everything seemed on the up and up. We certainly didn't see any men with cuts on their faces.

At the end of our third aisle, I pressed my fist into the small of my back and stretched. Bending over tables and looking at diamonds all morning was hard work!

Elijah came to a stop beside me, lips turned down in frustration. His gaze skimmed over the remaining aisles that we hadn't gotten to yet. "Who knew there were so many diamond dealers in the US?"

"I know, right?" I followed his gaze. "It would help if we had even a hint of an idea where to start."

He gave me a sardonic smirk. He swept a gesture to the three aisles we had just completed. "Well, we know we don't need to start anywhere in this area."

I snickered. At least if we were hitting dead ends, we were hitting them together. "Next aisle?"

The Ladies Room

ELIJAH SHOOK HIS HEAD. "I'm starving. Let's grab some lunch first."

Several food vendors were set up on one side of the huge warehouse, and while we headed that way, I called Colleen. "We are stopping for lunch. You guys want to join us?"

"I think so. One sec." She said something muffled to Garrett and then came back with, "Yeah, we'll meet you by the food."

Miraculously there was a table for four available as we approached the raised seating area. Three stairs led us up to the tables.

Elijah tugged out one of the chairs. "We better grab this while we can. You want to sit while I order?"

"Sure." Not gonna lie. It felt wonderful to sink into that hard plastic chair.

Elijah skimmed the vendors. "What do you want? Looks like tacos, burgers, Thai, or Italian."

"It all sounds good."

He looked down at me, one brow lifted.

"Really. I'm not just saying that. I'm an adventurous eater. Whatever you want, just get two and I'll be happy."

"An adventurous eater who doesn't eat veggies?"

I waved a hand. "I eat plenty of veggies. Chocolate grows on trees, you know."

He barked a laugh. "Burger and fries with a Coke?"

"Sounds perfect."

"Be right back."

While Elijah stood in line at the burger place, I turned my attention to the remainder of the room. Since the tables were on a low platform, I had a better view of the warehouse. But after only a moment, I realized with a sigh that it wasn't going to help me any. The place was quite literally a sea of booths. It would be a miracle if we discovered any clues here today.

Colleen and Garrett stopped by and dropped Colleen's coat on the chair next to mine, but then they strode off together to the Italian place.

Elijah returned a moment later and set a tray with a huge burger and mound of orange sweet-potato fries in front of me. The Coke was so huge there was no way I'd be able to drink even a quarter of it. Across the table from me, his tray held two ramekins of a white sauce and he transferred one of them to my tray. "You've got to try the sweet-potato fries dipped in buttermilk ranch." He pumped his brows.

"Sounds amazing."

We both bowed our heads for a short grace, and then dove into our food. After one bite of a fry dipped in the ranch, I rolled my eyes in ecstasy. "This is amazing!"

Elijah was concentrating on his own fries. He gave me a nod, and then a bit of a frown settled between his brows. "What did you need to see Jason about at the station the other day? We've been so swamped that I keep forgetting to ask him."

"Oh, that was about Mom. And Marnie, too, I guess." I filled him in on the kitten scam.

Elijah sank against his chair, food seemingly forgotten, even though he was holding a fry. "Huh. That makes three then because Maisy Simmons came by to tell us something similar happened to her. Only in her case, the cat she wanted cost five thousand, and she put down half."

"Half! She's the lady who owns Spritz or Dye, right?"

He nodded.

"Between the three of them, that's three thousand five hundred dollars! What if this guy is doing that in cities all over the country? I mean, it's the internet, right? He could be making tons of money."

Elijah's brow crimped. "They'd have to launder it somehow to make it look legit. I'll have to check with some other agencies to see if they've had similar reports."

"Like you didn't already have enough to worry about. I'm sorry."

His gaze zipped to mine. He studied me seriously for one moment before one side of his mouth lifted. "I kinda like having someone to feel sorry for me over how hard I work."

Colleen slid her tray into the spot next to mine. "How hard you work? You should see how hard your office-help works."

Her spaghetti looked amazing.

Elijah gave her an indulgent nod. "Noted. I'll be sure to remind your boss to give you time off when this case is finished. Did you guys see anything suspicious?"

Garrett sank into the chair beside Elijah. "Other than the outrageous prices on some of those pieces of jewelry? Nada."

Colleen leaned toward me. "We saw a necklace that was priced at half a million dollars! Can you imagine wearing that amount around your neck?!"

I could not.

But I was prevented from replying by Garrett's next words. "Then the next booth over had a necklace that was really similar, but they were only asking fifty thousand for it because it was made with lab-grown diamonds."

Elijah opened his mouth, but Colleen lifted a palm. "I know. But I didn't see anything suspicious about their booth. And none of the people had a healing cut on their face."

I looked at Elijah. "What are the chances that guy would be here? I mean, he sent his partner, or whatever

Kevin Swift was, after me, so he knows I was outside the boat. Maybe he's just staying hidden?"

"Could be. Our chances are pretty slim." His phone buzzed and he swiped to answer. "Hi, Jason. What's up?" He listened for a moment. "Yeah, Shelby was just filling me in on why she stopped to talk to you." He listened again for a few minutes. Suddenly, he straightened. "You're kidding me!"

Colleen and I exchanged a glance.

"No. No. You were right to call me with that." Another moment of silence. "Sure. Put him on. Hi, Auggy. Oh really? That's great work. No, I trust you. I'll take a look at the footage as soon as we get back."

After he hung up and set his phone on the table, it seemed to take him a few moments to realize we were all three staring at him. He dabbled a fry through his dressing. "Jason was able to trace the real address of the scammer through the PO box that he used to collect the money . . ."

"And?" I held my breath. Would Mom be able to get her money back?

"It was on Cormorant Island. The address belongs to a man named Kirk Canfield, according to the county register."

That set me back against my seat. "The cat guy lives on the same island as where the boat went?" That reminded me that I'd never asked Elijah what he and Jason had discovered on the island when they went back. But I had no time to voice my question because Elijah was still talking.

"And Auggy, bless him, has been able to restore most of the video from your phone. He says your instincts were right on the money. The name painted on the side of the boat from the pictures I took at Cormorant matches the one in your video."

My mind scrambled to put pieces together. It was like trying to do a puzzle without ever knowing what the original image looked like. There were lots of pieces, and a few were finally snapping together, but I couldn't quite get the whole picture figured out yet. Now was the chance for my question. "What did you and Jason find when you went back the other day?"

Elijah lifted one shoulder. "Not much more than I saw the first day. The boat was gone and the place remained tightly locked up. But the building looks like a big warehouse. Cement walls. No windows. Lots of steam coming out the top. Without a warrant we couldn't go inside, so we were only able to walk the grounds."

Lots of steam had to mean lots of electricity, right? "How much does it cost, do you think, to create a lab-grown diamond?"

Elijah studied me as though waiting for me to reveal more.

Colleen had a mouthful of spaghetti. She used a napkin to wipe her lips as she waggled her head to indicated she wasn't sure.

Garrett shrugged one shoulder. "Likely a whole lot less than setting up a mine."

"Yeah, but there would still be costs right? Electricity. Carbon. The pressurizing chambers. That kind of thing."

"Yeah," Elijah said cautiously. "What are you thinking?"

"The cats!"

Elijah frowned, holding yet another uneaten fry.

Colleen and Garrett only looked at me like I'd lost my mind.

"What cats?" Colleen asked.

I filled her in then turned my focus back to Elijah. "It was what you said about laundering the money to make it legit."

"Shelby, you're a genius," Elijah beamed.

"I'm lost," Garrett said.

I set my tray to one side and leaned forward, excited at all the possibilities pumping through my head.

"Say you need some startup money to get into a very lucrative diamond business. So you set up a scam to 'sell' kittens that you never have plans to deliver. You could advertise the kittens all over in whatever city you want. You'd only have to do a little research to make the victims at ease that you really are from their area and are a legit person. The victims mail the down-payment for the kittens to your PO box—which, let's face it, seems pretty dumb, but people who want something bad enough are often willing to take risks. And what is a more emotional purchase than that of buying a pet? Anyhow, you—the scammer—collect the money and use it for your startup of a diamond-growing lab."

Elijah was frowning. "But it can take weeks to grow a diamond. So all of that would have needed to happen weeks ago. And your mom, Marnie, and Maisy were only scammed this past week."

"Maybe it wasn't just start-up money. Maybe he's running the kitten scam continually—could be fake-selling any kind of pet or anything, really—and using the diamond sales to wash the illegal money brought in from the kittens?"

Colleen twisted her lips to one side. "This all seems pretty far-fetched."

"Yeah, it kind of does," I admitted. "Also, it would be pretty dumb to run the kitten scam in your own hometown. Seems like something he would have done in faraway cities with PO boxes forwarding to other boxes to hide his trail."

Garrett shrugged. "Unless he needed some fast cash. Mailing to a local box would get him some money quicker than if he had to wait for it to filter through a series of forwards from other PO boxes.

"That's true." Elijah offered. "But it wouldn't explain why the diamonds were hidden inside fish."

I sat back. No. It wouldn't. "It was a really far-fetched idea, anyhow. I mean, how likely is it that someone could really make that much money on scamming people with pet purchases?"

Elijah lifted a shoulder. "It never hurts to explore every avenue of possibility. In fact . . ." He lifted his phone and dialed, leaving us all hanging.

"Auggy? Do me a favor? I know we already took a look at all the inhabitants of Cormorant Island, but cross check that with any information Jason has on this kitten scam situation would you? You can leave your findings on my desk. I'd like to give everything another look this evening when I get home."

After he hung up, we all finished our food and then Elijah and I parted ways with Garrett and Colleen to resume visiting the booths.

After another five hours, an announcer came over the sound system to announce that we had thirty minutes to vacate the building, and to thank us all for our attendance. We wandered a few more booths, foot-weary and depressed at our lack of discovery. In the middle of that row, there was a space with a table, but no one had set up a display. For some reason, the sight bumped up my pulse rate.

"What happened to this booth?" I asked the woman who manned the slot next to the empty one.

She shrugged. "Someone was supposed to be here, but never showed up. Kind of crazy because these booths cost us practically and arm and a leg."

While Elijah continued to chat with the woman, I meandered over to the empty table. In the middle of it was a taped-down paper with instructions to the vendor. When I saw the name of the business, my heart really did start pumping in earnest. "Elijah?"

When he looked up, I motioned him over. I held up the paper for him to see.

"Salish Serenade," he muttered, reading, "Diamonds grown in the heart of the San Juans."

"Interesting, right?"

Elijah flicked the corner of the page as he thoughtfully stared into the distance. "Very."

"What do you think it means?"

He looked back to me and lifted one shoulder. "Could mean any number of things, but what it likely means is that the man we are looking for didn't show his face today."

Disappointment sagged my shoulders. "That's what I was afraid of." A sigh of frustration puffed through my lips. I had really hoped that this diamond expo would give us some leads.

With only fifteen minutes left to vacate the building, we decided it was time to go. Elijah snapped a picture of the page and then called Colleen to let her know to meet us at Garrett's car.

I had a need of the ladies room, so I told Elijah that I required a moment.

He nodded. "Me too. Meet you back at this bench?"

The wooden bench sat against one wall of the warehouse near the little hallway that led to the restrooms. I gave him a thumbs-up. "Back in five."

The short hallway from the warehouse floor teed into another hallway with signs that directed people to the bathrooms. Men to the left, women to the right. The fluorescent lights in the hallway flickered and hummed as I pushed through the women's restroom door. Several other ladies had beat me inside and the last stall door was just closing when I entered. A woman stood at the sinks, washing her hands. I tried not to dance like a little girl as I waited for a stall to become available.

As I looked around, I realized that the bathroom was fancy for being in a warehouse. They probably used this building for large conferences from time to time. The stall dividers were floor to ceiling and made of some type of beautifully grained wood. Each stall door was made of a single thick piece of the same wood, and the handles were sturdy U-shaped bars that looked like they might have been crafted in the Middle Ages by some brawny blacksmith. A frilly palm sat in one corner of the room with two delicate white chairs on either side. Elevator music pumped through speakers inset into the ceiling, and near the sinks, as the woman shook water from her hands, air freshener spritzed from a motion-detector-unit on the wall. The room was a contrast in old-world and Victorian decor that somehow melded into a beautiful ambiance that relaxed and soothed.

But I still needed a stall, stat.

As more women—one of them on crutches with her foot in a big black boot, poor thing—pushed through the door behind me, I felt grateful to at least be at the front of the line. Finally, there came the wondrous sound of a muffled flush, and a stall door opened a couple inches, but then fell closed again. No one emerged.

I rolled my eyes. Likely someone had forgotten to zip, or realized their skirt was off kilter.

The door popped open a second time. But again, only a few inches before it slammed shut.

I frowned. A rattling, clattery sound like metal tapping on wood emerged, but the door remained closed.

The woman in line behind me leaned to peer around me.

We exchanged a puzzled glance.

I stepped forward. "Do you need some help in there?"

A soft-spoken crackly voice said, "Yes! Please could you open the door for me? It's so heavy."

I hauled on the handle, and the woman wasn't wrong. That door might as well have weighed nine hundred pounds!

When I got the door open, a tiny elderly woman with a poof of white curls surrounding her head looked up at me. She wasn't much bigger than a teacup and was leaning on a walker.

No wonder the poor woman had been having a hard time escaping her stall.

Her eyes were a startling blue when she smiled. "Thank you so much. I thought I might be stuck in here forever." She laughed.

I smiled. "That wouldn't be any fun. Especially since they certainly didn't make these stalls any bigger than a tissue box, did they? Here, let me hold the door for you."

I pressed my back to the door and braced my feet, the hinges fighting me the whole time. "Man, what were they trying to build in here? A prison?"

She laughed again. "Could be! Thank you, dear. I appreciate your help."

"Not a problem."

I waited patiently for her to maneuver her walker past me and get to the sink. And was relieved (no pun intended) to finally be able to enter the stall. I have to say that while the ambiance worked on the room in general, the stalls were really dark and the fully enclosed space left me feeling claustrophobic. I supposed it was considered more posh to have a floor-to-ceiling division between the stalls, but I felt a bit like the walls were closing in on me. I would not think of mortuaries or body-storage drawers! I simply wouldn't.

Drops of sweat formed on my brow.

Sweet mercy, I needed to get out of here.

I flung my bag onto the brass hook on the door. I'd only been in there for thirty seconds when the elevator music stopped and an announcement blared over the speakers.

"The warehouse doors will be locked in five minutes. Please vacate the building immediately. The expo will resume tomorrow morning at ten."

Had I really been waiting out there in the main part of the bathroom for over ten minutes? I hurried to finish and was just reaching for my bag so I could leave when I heard a thunk on the door of my stall. "I'm coming. Sorry. I know it's been a bit of a wait."

Bag over my shoulder, I slid the lock open and pressed the door.

It didn't budge.

I rolled my eyes. Stupid heavy door. I pushed with all my might.

Not even a smidge of movement.

I pressed again, still to no avail. And that was when it hit me!

That thump I'd heard . . . Had someone jammed my door somehow to lock me in?

That Close to Escape

ONE HAND TO MY chest, I willed myself not to panic. I spun in a circle, scrutinizing the whole stall. But it was just as I'd originally thought. Sturdy floor-to-ceiling walls with no way of escape other than the little inset fan in the ceiling and I'd have to be Lilliputian to fit through that.

I tried the door again—okay, maybe several times—and finally gave up. "Hello? Is anyone out there?"

I was greeted with nothing but silence.

"Please, can anyone let me out of here?"

More silence.

Elijah! I was fumbling through my purse for my phone when all the lights snapped off. I froze, heart thumping in my throat.

If I thought I'd been sweating before, I was really sweating now. I pulled in a deliberately long breath and pushed it out through pursed lips. Tried to imagine open fields with green grass and white daisies wafting in a breeze. The picture wouldn't form.

Do not panic. Do not panic!

I forced myself to concentrate on feeling the items in my purse. Mom had a special pocket in her purse where she always put her phone. Why, oh why, didn't I have that same habit? But no. I had to be the type of person who simply tossed her phone into her bag and let it land where it may.

I found one firm rectangular shape, but quickly realized that it was the business card holder Mom had gotten me for my B&B cards, and not my phone.

After fumbling my way through two more compartments, I almost sobbed when my fingers finally latched onto my phone. I swiped the screen and wanted to hug the inventor of back-lit screens when the stall illuminated with the soft light. I was so thankful that all my contacts had been added when I'd purchased my phone at the store.

I pressed Elijah's name, pushing away the niggle of embarrassment over the teasing I was going to receive from him for this.

"Shelby? Where are you?"

"I'm still in the bathroom. Someone locked me in."

"What?!" I heard a horn honk in the background.

No! That meant . . . "Are you outside?"

"Shelby, are you alone?"

"Yes, I'm alone! I'm locked in a freaking bathroom stall that looks like it was built to keep knights imprisoned! Tell me you didn't go outside without me?!"

I could hear his footsteps slapping against the ground. His breath puffed in my ear. "It took me forever in the men's room because it was so busy. When I came out, a woman by the bench told me that you wanted me to meet you at the car. So I came outside. Hold on." His next words were muffled and far away. "Excuse me? Are you with security? I need to get back inside. A friend has been locked in the women's restroom."

"What? Not possible," a male voice responded. "We did a sweep. Only the security team is allowed to be inside now."

"I'm telling you, I've got her on the phone. She says someone has locked her into one of the stalls."

"You're kidding me?"

"Do I look like I'm kidding?" There was the sound of shuffling and then, "I'm Sheriff Elijah Gains of the San Juan Island Sheriff's Department. This is my badge. I was here today investigating a case that I've been working on, and my . . . associate . . . is still inside."

Aw. Despite my circumstances, my insides went a little gooey. He'd called me his associate? Just having Elijah as close as the other end of a phone connection had calmed me considerably.

That was when I heard voices coming down the hall.

My eyes shot wide and I tightened my grip just in time to keep from dropping my phone.

The outer door of the bathroom squeaked open. "You sure you got her?"

My mouth fell open. It was the voice of the man that I'd heard in the argument at the marina the other day, I felt certain of it.

"One hundred percent. Locked her in the stall with the crutch just like you said." That was a woman's voice that I didn't recognize. "I'll take that money now."

My mouth fell open. Some woman—presumably the one who'd come in behind me on crutches—had taken money to lock me in this stall?

The man blew out a breath of annoyance, but not long after that, I heard the sound of paper *scritch*ing against paper.

"Thank you very much," the woman said. And then the bathroom door squeaked open and shut again.

I was alone in the bathroom with a man who likely wanted me dead considering he'd sent his goon after me at the marina!

I had to think!

As quietly as I could, I slid the lock back into place. But it was only about a quarter of an inch of metal and wasn't going to hold anyone out for long.

God, please let Elijah get here in time!

I pressed the volume button down to the lowest level so that if Elijah talked it wouldn't be heard, then carefully slid my phone into an outer pocket of my bag so it wouldn't hang up. I wanted Elijah to be able to hear what was going on without giving away my presence.

I settled the strap more firmly on my shoulder. My panicked gaze swept around the interior of the stall. There was absolutely nothing in here with which to protect myself. I mean, what was I going to do? Whack the guy with the extra TP roll? There wasn't even a tank lid to use as a weapon because the toilet was one of those fancy kinds where the pipes went straight into the walls and it flushed itself when you moved.

The man tapped on the door. "Hello? I hear you've been looking for me."

I maintained my silence. Maybe he'd think the girl had made a mistake and walk away. Yeah, right.

"Surprise," he singsonged. "I'm right here. Why don't you come out and we can talk, hmm?"

I scrambled up to balance on the toilet. It flushed.

On the other side of the door, the man chuckled.

I rolled my eyes. So much for maintaining my silence. I faced the door, and braced my hands on either wall. Whatever was about to happen, I didn't plan to go down without a fight.

"Kind of quiet for a girl who likes to snoop in others' business and talk to the cops so much."

I readied myself to kick out with both feet as soon as that door budged even the slightest.

"Your snooping got me into some hot water. And cost me my best friend."

His best friend? Kevin Swift? The goon who stabbed Anthony for picking up the wrong cooler? Had to be him, right?

"Telling them about his island lab really wasn't very kind of you."

Interesting. If Kevin Swift was really who he'd hinted at earlier, that meant that Kevin was connected to the lab. "His lab," as in, he owned it? Or "his lab" as in he simply worked there? Had to be that he owned it, right? After all, you wouldn't say "his store" about someone who simply worked at a store. I tucked that bit of information away to ponder some more.

Despite the earlier flush, I was still of no mind to confirm my presence in the stall, so maintained my silence.

From the other side of the door, the man chuckled, then the horrifying sound of an electric saw started up!

A thin blade slid through the crack where the door met the doorpost and then disappeared into a blur as the motor on the saw ramped up another notch. Sparks flew and a metallic screech filled the room the moment the blade reached the little strap of metal that was currently the only thing keeping me safe. I wouldn't be safe for long. Elijah wasn't going to get here in time!

I'm sure you've heard the saying that the best prayers you pray are when you are upside down in a well? Yeah. Let me just say that you can also do some pretty good praying when you are locked in a bathroom stall while some guy with a saw works to get at you! I only wished I could be confident that God was hearing little old me begging Him to intervene on my behalf.

I prepared myself for the moment that the lock would give way, watching the sparks continue to fly as the blade cut through the latch.

Just when I was sure he was through, the saw emitted a loud squawk and came to a halt. Black smoke drifted through the crack in the door.

The man cursed and jerked the blade free. He gave the door handle a couple of firm yanks, but there was still enough of the latch in place to keep the door shut.

My hopes soared.

Maybe Elijah would be able to get here in time, after all.

I could hear my captor grumbling and mumbling as he fiddled with his saw on the other side of the door. And it came to me with sudden realization that maybe if I got him talking, that would slow him down even more.

"So Kevin Swift owned the diamond lab on Cormorant Island?"

All sound from the other side of the door stopped. Then he said, "Ah, she speaks."

I waited, hoping he would answer, but to no avail.

After a long pause, he set to working on his saw again.

"Is your name Kirk Canfield?"

There was a hiss of pain and then a sound like someone sucking on a sliced finger. I presumed my question had startled him so much that he'd cut his finger on the saw. Which likely meant I was right. This was the guy who had been scamming women out of money for kittens. But . . . my brain hurt. What was the piece of the puzzle that I was missing here?

"Why were the diamonds inside fish, Kirk?"

Silence fell again for a heavy moment on the other side of the door.

"That's the piece of the puzzle that doesn't seem to fit, you know? I'm just wondering about the cooler of fish. After all, that was what started this whole murder spree, wasn't it?" I scrunched my nose and bit my lower lip. I probably shouldn't be so bold with only a partial piece of metal keeping me safe from this guy. But I wanted to give Elijah time to get here. I hoped he was still listening on my phone, but I didn't dare check in with him.

"Murder spree?" The man laughed sardonically. "I take exception to that." He worked at his saw, tools clicking and rattling.

"Well . . . first you, or Kevin, your 'best friend' as you called him, killed Anthony. And then you killed Kevin, presumably so he wouldn't talk to us—uh, to law enforcement. So yeah, I'd call that a spree. Especially for our area."

"I didn't kill—Listen, if you think I'm one of those dumb criminals who is going to brag about his feats, you're wrong. The only thing I'm going to say is that I haven't killed anyone! I'm not in this for the ego. Just the money. Now shut up."

Disappointment shot through me. It was really frustrating me that all the pieces of the puzzle seemed to be on the table, but I couldn't get them to fit together.

Then his words struck me. "You didn't kill Kevin? If you didn't kill him, who did?"

Silence.

I really wanted to peek through the crack in the door to see what he looked like or might be doing, but at any moment, he could thrust his saw back through that crack and I didn't relish a blade to my eye. Also, I didn't want to give up my high ground. So I stayed where I was.

"Earlier you said I cost you your best friend. I thought you meant I forced you to kill him. But now you are saying you didn't kill him?" My brain ached as I tried to connect all the dots. "If you didn't kill him, who did? Had to be someone with either law-enforcement or military experience, I think. Because that shot was one in a million." I was just rattling off stuff to fill time and disobey him now. Maybe I could get on his nerves enough to distress him into making a mistake. "So you're not a military man?"

More silence. Only some more tool clanking and another curse.

Okay . . . What now? "What do you want with me anyhow? I mean, I don't know anything really. Whatever went down is beyond me."

"Shut up, lady. I liked you better when you were quiet."

The saw started up, sending my heart into overdrive. A blade slid through the crack, this one shiny and new. That horrifying metal on metal sound once more filled the stall and I knew I was done for.

Elijah hadn't made it in time. What was taking him so dang long, anyhow?

I watched in horror as the new saw blade cut through the remainder of the flimsy lock like butter. The lock gave way. The screeching sounds stopped. The sparks quit flying.

I knew I only had one chance and I had to make it good.

Pressing my hands to either side of the stall, I braced myself and kicked that heavy door with both feet and all my might. It shot forward like the battering ram I'd hoped it would be.

There was a hollow *thunk* and then the door bounced closed again. I leapt down from the toilet and shoved through the portal, registering a large shadow bent over the sink, clutching his face.

I angled a sharp left and sprinted for the outer door.

It burst open before I was halfway there!

"Police! Get down! Get down!" Two policemen in tactical gear surged through the door, big black guns at the ready before them.

With a squeak of surprise, I thrust my hands in the air and dropped to my knees, not wanting to get shot by my rescuers.

Elijah stepped in right behind them, sweeping the room with his gun. His eyes shot wide. "Shelby! Watch out!"

An arm snaked around my neck and cold metal pressed to my temple.

My eyes fell closed, even as I fought to work my hands between his arm and my neck to get a little air. I'd been *that* close to escape.

Now I had a gun pointed at my head.

The Thing That I Know

ELIJAH REMAINED CENTER, WHILE the other two cops stepped to his right and left. I didn't recognize them. They must be from here in Seattle. Elijah must have asked for some backup.

In this tiny space, there wasn't much room for the officers to spread out, so everyone stilled—me and my captor on one end of the sink counter, and Elijah and the officers on the other.

Elijah's gaze drilled into mine over his gun barrel. "Shelby, breathe. Just breathe. I've got you."

I was trying, but let me tell you, whoever the guy was who had a hold of me, Kirk Canfield or someone else, he had a grip like a steel band. And all of it was currently focused on squeezing the life out of me.

"I'll kill her, I swear I will," the voice grated in my ear.

"She's the only thing keeping you alive right now. Best you remember that." Elijah's gun, shifted half an inch to one side. "What do you want with her?"

"I wanted my diamonds back, but she's just proven that she knows too much."

I shook my head, then froze as I realized that wasn't such a great idea when there was a gun to your temple. "I don't know anything!"

"Shut up," the voice snapped. To Elijah he said, "Right now, I'll settle for you simply letting me go."

"We can work that out."

"Sure, you can," the man snarled. "Don't you think I know that my back is against the wall here? If my saw hadn't jammed, we'd have been long gone by the time you got back in here."

My eyes fell closed as conviction washed through me. God *had* heard my prayer and had broken his blade, allowing Elijah to get here. Except . . .

God? Did You forget to take into consideration this part where I have a gun to my head?

"I've got a shot," the officer on my left said quietly as he sighted down his long black weapon of death. "Just let me know if you want me to take it."

I felt my captor tremble. He shuffled his feet and scooted us back a little. But I felt the bump as we came up against the wall.

The officer's shoulder connected with the stalls as he moved to keep my captor in his sights. "Still have a shot," he offered casually. "Might only blow part of his skull off, and he'll probably die in agony after a long wallow on the floor, but I've still got the shot."

"All right. All right. All right. I'll let her go. But I've got information, and I'm willing to talk so don't shoot me, okay? Only you have to promise me protection!"

Elijah's gaze glittered blue ice. "Let's just take this slow. If you do everything right, you'll be fine. But if you try anything, you're going down, understand?" The man must have nodded because Elijah continued, "Okay, good. Put your gun on the counter and slide it toward me."

My knees almost gave out from under me when my captor slowly pulled the gun away from my head and did as Elijah said.

"Good. You have any other weapons?"

"No. None." The man's voice trembled.

"Hands in the air then."

The arm around my throat released me and my legs were so weak that I almost couldn't stumble forward to meet Elijah, but I managed it.

He caught me to him with one arm, while keeping his gun trained on the man behind me.

There were the sounds of shuffling as the two Seattle officers yelled orders at the man and spun him around and cuffed his hands. Elijah waited only long enough to see that the job was done before hurrying me out of the room.

Out in the hallway, he held me for a brief moment, but then to my surprise he pressed me up against the wall and propped one hand beside my head, glowering down at me. "Apparently you know something you haven't been telling me?"

My jaw dropped open. Anger, hot and sure, surged. "Are you kidding me? I don't know anything more than what I've told you! Well, and . . . Were you able to hear our conversation over the phone?"

"I was, but . . ." His gaze narrowed on me. "He said you know too much."

"He might think that, but I assure you he is wrong! The only new thing I figured out is that he's the kitten scammer guy. Well, and that Kevin Swift was apparently his best friend and that Kevin likely owns the diamond lab, or at the very least was very high up in the ownership." A new thought registered then. "I bet Kirk is the owner of Salish Serenade! *That* would explain the fish!"

Elijah maintained his scrutiny, eyes hard and searching. Then his expression softened. "It would explain the fish, that's true."

"Also, he's crazy!" I rubbed my temple where the gun had been pressed only moments ago. "In case you may have forgotten."

With a sigh, he pushed away from me. He paced a couple of steps, scooping both hands back through his hair, and then gripping his neck before he retraced his steps to stop before me. "I haven't forgotten." He drew me into a much too short hug before he released me and said, "Come on, let's get you to Garrett and Colleen. They'll take you home. I'm going to have to stay here and deal with the interrogation and the paperwork on this arrest. You okay?"

A chill swept through me and I folded my arms against it as I kept pace by Elijah's side. "Yeah. I'm fine," I lied.

Elijah didn't look convinced, but he let it slide. He escorted me to where Garrett and Colleen waited in the parking lot and then turned and walked away without anything more than a wave of farewell.

Colleen yanked me into a firm embrace. "What happened? All we heard was Elijah yelling about the fact that you'd been locked inside."

I pulled in a steadying breath, relishing the feel of friendly arms around me—such a contrast to those of moments ago. "Some guy locked me in the bathroom. He said I knew too much, and I think he was planning to kill me, but Elijah and the officers got there in time." I stepped back, looking toward the warehouse with a shiver.

"Who was it?"

I shook my head. "I'm not sure. I never even saw his face. But I think it was Kirk Canfield."

"The pet-scammer guy is a psychopathic murderer?" Her tone was incredulous.

I only looked at her until she flapped a hand. "Right. It doesn't matter. That must have been terrifying! Are you okay?"

I swept a strand of windswept hair behind my ear. "I don't have any desire to experience that again, but I'm fine."

She gave me another squeeze. "Come on, let's get you home." Colleen nudged me to the car's back door that Garrett held open.

I sank into the backseat and shut the door with a great deal of relief to be leaving Seattle behind.

All of us were pretty quiet on the ride home. Garrett and Colleen were probably being quiet to give me some space, but I was racking my brain, trying to come up with some reason why I kept finding myself in severely hot water so often over the past few months. Maybe I needed to simply become a recluse.

By the time Garrett pulled into the B&B driveway to drop me off, I had a massive headache. I hugged Mom, assured her that I was fine and that I thought we may have caught the man who had ripped her off, and then I begged off to my room.

Ah the sweet scent of soft soil turned beneath my spade. Cherub faces of pansies, violas, and English daisies arched toward the sun. Waxy, tight-budded begonias, and heart-shaped cyclamen snuggled next to bunchgrass and lemon cypress. I stood back, fingernails coated in earth, the creases of my palm like an etched map, and I sighed, satisfied. Gardening did wonders for my soul.

It had been two days since I'd last seen Elijah. Two days where my thoughts kept spinning and my headache never abated. Even now, here in my happy place, it plagued me and raised my irritation.

I gathered my spade and claw, dropped them into my gardening bucket, and then stomped over to grab the hose, rinse my hands, and then water the hanging baskets in front of the garage.

Elijah pulled into our drive.

Drat if my heart didn't skip a beat the moment I heard the sound of his truck. I was still a little mad at him for coming at me like he had after my capture, and it made me even madder that my dang heart hadn't seemed to get on board with my peeve.

He climbed from the truck, wearing rough-worn blue jeans and a pair of cowboy boots that could fairly make a girl drool—if, you know, she wasn't still mad at him. The sleeves on his button-up blue shirt were rolled to just below his elbows, revealing the bronze cords of muscular arms—and emphasizing the blue of his gaze that swept me with a searching scrutiny.

I lifted my chin and spun away to wind the hose back onto its reel.

Elijah's boots sounded on the pavement behind me and stopped by my side.

I ignored him and kept cranking.

He took me gently by one arm and urged me to stand.

With a huff, I let go of the handle and allowed him to tug me around to face him. He remained close, the warmth of him pressed up against me as he touched my chin with the knuckle of his first finger, and eased my back against the garage door.

Let me tell you, my knees were glad for the reprieve. I swallowed. Wanted to look away, but somehow couldn't bring myself to break our connection.

"I'm an idiot, Shel. I shouldn't have talked to you like that. I was hopped up on adrenaline and terror." His thumb stroked my chin.

Yeah. When he put it like that, I guess I had been too.

"Forgive me?"

I toyed with making him grovel a little longer, but then my traitorous gaze dipped to those soft lips of his that were nestled in the middle of a day or two's worth of stubble, and heat flashed through my face. I tore my focus back to his. "O-of course."

Nice, Shelby. Way to sound real forgiving.

I pulled in a breath. "I mean, yes. No problem. We were both understandably a little tense and—"

Elijah's face dipped closer. His mouth hovered above mine, just long enough to give me time to pull away, if I wanted to. I didn't want to. And then his lips settled against mine, soft and gentle, maybe even a bit tentative. He immediately started to ease back, but I leaned after him, not content with such a brief moment of contact.

The kiss was all that I had hyped it up to be in my mind over the last few weeks of knowing this man— and more. So. Much. More. My fingers found their way into the soft curls at his neck. I felt the warmth of his hand slip around to my back. He tasted like mint and contentment. I released a blissful sigh against his mouth.

And then a man behind Elijah cleared his throat rather pointedly.

Elijah lifted his head, leaving me feeling cold and barren. He stepped back with a bit of a grin as he pressed the pad of his thumb across his lips. "Did I forget to mention that I asked Jason to join me here this morning to talk to you?"

My gaze shot past Elijah's shoulder to see Jason, wearing his uniform, standing in the driveway by his cruiser. I hadn't even heard the vehicle pull up.

With a bit of a devilish grin, Jason tugged on the brim of his hat. "Shelby."

Was my face as red as the heat shooting through my cheeks made me suspect that it was?

"Morning." I tried to sound calm, and failed miserably. "Please come in, both of you. Last night was the first night in weeks that we didn't have a guest, so Mom and I are taking it a bit easy this morning."

Speaking of Mom . . . She was going to downright have a coronary because when I'd come out to water the plants, she'd still been in the kitchen with curlers in her hair—yes, Mom was still a throwback to the eighties, though thankfully, she'd updated her hairstyle to a wavy cut that did wonders for her cheekbones.

Jason stepped past us. "I'll just mosey in and chat with your mom for a few minutes, while you two finish . . . talking, out here." He grinned and winked as he passed us.

I held out one finger. "Maybe I should—" But I was prevented from hurrying past Jason into the house, when Elijah reached out to clasp my hand and tugged me back against his chest.

"Now where were we," he rumbled.

I felt a flush of warmth surge through me, but I really did need to rescue Mom, so I held up one finger before Elijah could kiss me once again. "Tempting as it would be to stand out here with you all day, Mom is still in her curlers."

For a moment, his brow crimped and then his gaze shot toward Jason, who was just stepping up onto the porch. "Oh! Hey, Jason?"

The undersheriff spun back our way. "Yeah?"

"Need to talk to you for one minute."

"Sure, boss." Jason returned our direction. "What is it?"

I shot onto my tiptoes and kissed Elijah's cheek. Then I reluctantly let go of his hand and hurried past Jason and into the house.

Mom was tooling around the kitchen in her robe. "Hi hon, the crepe batter is all mixed up and I was just waiting for you to come inside to start fry—"

"Mom, Jason is right outside with Elijah and they want to talk to us for a few minutes." I raised my brows, waiting for the explosion.

"Jason? Right out—Oh land almighty, Shelby!" She threw her hands to the curlers in her hair. "Well, I'm still—I've still got—And—" her gesture swept around the kitchen at the mess she'd made while making our lazy-day breakfast.

I grabbed her shoulders. "Elijah is stalling him a bit. Go upstairs. I'll clean this up and then we can fry crepes for everyone." I shoved her toward the stairs.

She ran like I hadn't seen her run in years, snatching curlers from her hair as she went, and eliciting a laugh from me as I scrambled to swipe the counters and toss dishes into the dishwasher. I shoved the basket of our personal laundry that we'd planned to do today into the laundry room just as the doorbell rang.

I quickly washed my hands and then, nonchalantly, opened the front door as if this was the first time I was seeing Elijah this morning. "Why Sheriff, how lovely to see you." I infused my best southern drawl into the words. "And Undersheriff White! Do come in. Mom is just upstairs and will be down shortly. We were just making crepes, can I tempt you boys into breakfast?"

Elijah chuckled and hooked his thumbs into his back pockets. "Sounds good to me. Jason?"

There was a twinkle in the older man's eyes as he nodded. "Sound deliciou—" His gaze snagged on something behind me and he snatched his hat from his head.

I turned to see Mom, breezing down the stairs in a figure-hugging sheath-dress that came to just above her knees. She'd slipped on a cute pair of Mary Janes and even had lipstick and mascara on. Not a hair was out of place.

I shook my head a little. I didn't know how she did it, but she looked like an older model just stepping from the pages of a magazine.

Undersheriff White swallowed and twisted his hat through his fingers. "M-morning, Ms. Stewart."

Mom waved a hand. "Please. All my friends call me Wanda, as I've told you before. And I do consider you a friend. Now, are you boys hungry?"

"I could eat, yes, ma'am," Elijah offered.

Jason only nodded, seemingly unable to take his eyes off my mom.

I grinned.

Mom smoothed her hands over her dress and swept toward the kitchen. "Good. Right this way. I'm making crepes. Who wants coffee?"

I brought up the rear. "Why don't we eat on the patio, Mom?"

"That sounds perfect."

I got the men coffee and set the table on our fitted-stone patio while Mom commenced frying the crepes. They only took about a minute a piece, and by the time I'd added the syrup, jam, butter, and Mom's special blintz filling, along with a big bowl of fresh raspberries, Mom was settling a platter of the thin pancakes on the table and easing gracefully into her seat.

I shut Kodi in the house so he wouldn't pester us with his begging. From behind the glass of the door, he looked at me like I was the meanest human being this side of Africa.

Mom asked Jason to say grace, and as he murmured a heartfelt prayer, I suddenly was filled with curiosity over what had brought them both here this morning.

Jason was in his uniform, but Elijah was not, which meant it likely wasn't an official visit? Or was it?

Someone snapped their fingers and I jerked my head up, realizing that I'd wool-gathered the prayer time away and all three of them were looking at me with amusement in their eyes.

"Sorry. I was just trying to figure out what brought you both here?"

"The company of two beautiful ladies isn't a good enough excuse?" Elijah asked.

I laughed. "Except, Jason is in uniform, which makes me wonder if this is some sort of an official visit?"

Jason watched Mom carefully as she assembled a crepe and then copied her actions. "Elijah is here officially too, only he's put in so much overtime lately, that he's supposed to be taking a day off." The older man's gaze flashed to his boss in fatherly irritation.

"As soon as this case is wrapped, I'm hoping to do just that." Elijah filled his crepe with peanut butter and rolled it up. He drizzled syrup along the length of it. "Which I'm hoping we can take care of this morning."

"Oh?" I scooped blintz filling and raspberries into mine. "Did you learn anything more from that man?"

"We did."

"Who he is?"

Elijah swallowed a bite and took a sip of coffee before he replied, "His name is Kirk Canfield, just as we suspected. Oh, and . . ." He dug into his back pocket and withdrew an envelope. He plopped it on the table next to Mom's plate. "We got your money back."

"You did?" Mom gasped. "Oh, I'm so relieved!" She opened the envelope and I caught a glimpse of several one-hundred-dollar bills.

"So he *was* the kitten scammer guy?"

Elijah nodded.

"I'm so confused. Why did he want to kidnap me?"

Elijah held up one hand. "Let me start from the beginning."

"Please do," Mom said.

"Apparently, Kevin Swift and Kirk Canfield were buddies, growing up. It seems Kirk was a bit of a no-good drifter who would rather smoke marijuana and lie around his house all day. But his buddy, Kevin, a go-getter, started the diamond-growing lab with some inheritance money. Anyhow, according to Kirk, he just sort of stumbled into the pet-scam business. He needed money one day and put up his first fake ad. He was surprised at how much money he made, and it was all downhill from there. We seized his assets. In addition to the multi-million-dollar home he bought on Cormorant, you'll never believe how much money he had in the bank."

"How much?"

Elijah looked to Jason, who set down his fork. "Nine hundred and thirty-seven thousand in round figures."

My fork clattered against my plate. "Mom, we're in the wrong business."

She snorted. "Shel Belle, neither of us ever want to end up on the bad side of these two lawmen."

"Well that's true . . . I guess."

Elijah smirked.

"So how do the diamonds come into this whole mess?" I asked. "And what about Anthony?"

"Well, when Kirk started making so much money from his little scam, he realized he needed a legitimate front to launder the money. He went to his buddy Kevin and offered to start buying diamonds, under the table. He even set up that cover company, Salish Serenade. Apparently he was selling for rock-bottom prices at diamond expos all across the country and then marking them up in his books, you know, to account for the pet scam's money."

I savored a creamy bite of blintz and raspberries before I asked, "So, if they lived next to each other on Cormorant, they could have simply exchanged money for diamonds on the island without drawing attention to themselves. Why then did they have a cooler full of fish stuffed with diamonds?"

"That's where it gets interesting." Jason lifted another crepe from the plate and set to filling it while Mom refilled our coffees.

Elijah leaned back and held his cup so Mom could easily reach it with the coffee pot. "Apparently the two of them had a third buddy growing up—Aaron King. One who is involved in a much less savory business, according to Kirk. One night down at the Lush Chaser,

Kirk got drunk and talked a little too liberally. The next day, their 'buddy,'" Elijah air quoted the phrase, "showed up, claiming that he'd out them both if they didn't help him with a little side hustle."

"What kind of a side hustle?" I asked.

Elijah and Jason shared a look. Then Elijah released a breath. "Kirk swears up and down that he doesn't know what it was. Just that he and Kevin were supposed to bring two thousand diamonds out to Crown Island and Aaron would meet them at the pier."

"With cash?"

Elijah shook his head. "The diamonds were payment for his silence."

I pulled a wow face. "I bet Kevin was none too happy with Kirk about that."

Elijah shook his head. "I don't know. Kirk seemed to think that Kevin knew more about Aaron's dealings than he wanted to say."

I pondered while I took a slow sip of coffee. "I guess that would explain him coming after me—Colleen and me—at the marina. I mean . . . if he had a bigger . . . I don't know what—crime syndicate?—to protect."

"Maybe," Elijah pushed back his plate.

"So we know that Kirk stabbed Anthony because he took the wrong cooler, the one with the diamonds. Did he admit to that?"

Elijah nodded. "He did."

"But Kevin wasn't happy with him being so stupid. He yelled at him that he should have just exchanged the coolers. Probably because he didn't want any undue attention on what was about to go down."

"Especially when it was so unnecessary." Jason pushed back his plate and rested one hand on his shirtfront. He looked at Mom. "Best breakfast I've had in eons."

Mom blushed. "Thank you."

"So Anthony's murder is solved, but leaves us—you two—with questions about the murder of Kevin Swift in your jail?"

"That about sums it up and is what brings us here." Elijah's hard gaze landed right on me.

My brows shot up. Here I'd thought we were simply having a nice breakfast and now he seemed to be mad at me about something—again. "What?!"

"According to Kirk, the boss of the crime syndicate is the one who sent him after you at the expo. He seems to be of the mind that you know too much."

"What? I don't know anything! Who is this boss of the crime syndicate?"

He shook his head with a sigh. "Kirk wouldn't say, and believe me, we tried to get it out of him. He said one peep would cost him his life. We assured him we'd keep him safe, but he said we wouldn't be able to. He just wants to do his time and then get on living. But he did say that when the boss met you, you seemed to know just a little too much."

"Met me?" My voice squeaked like a dog whose tail had just been stepped on. "I've never met any crime boss!"

Elijah reached over and covered my hand.

I snatched mine into my lap. "Seriously, I have not been holding out. I have no idea what he might be talking about!"

"Just think, Shelby. There has to be someone you've met that you haven't mentioned. Even a casual conversation you had with someone where you might have mentioned something about the case?"

I racked my mind. I truly did. But I couldn't come up with a single person that I'd spoken to, other than . . . My eyes shot wide and I lifted my head. "Your grandfather!"

"My grand—" Elijah seemed so shocked that he couldn't even finish the word.

Jason hooted! He slapped Elijah on the shoulder. "Your grandfather!" He laughed some more. "Just wait until we tell the old coot that the girl you're interested in suspects him of being the boss of a crime syndicate."

By this time, Elijah was laughing and I realized that his shock was more one of denial than of agreement with my accusation.

I have to admit that I was a little peeved at their humor. "What?" I snapped. "I mean, it could be possible. He was in law enforcement, so he would have the connections to know what cell Kevin was in, and he could be a crack shot. Is he? A crack shot?"

Elijah seemed to have sobered some. He shook his head thoughtfully. "Not good enough to take that shot at Kevin."

"Well, he might know someone who was a good enough shot to have killed Kevin in his cell."

"You're barking up the wrong tree, Shelby," Jason said. "I've known Mac my whole life and worked with him from the day I started my career until he resigned a few years ago. He'd never do something like this."

"Well . . ." I leaned into the back of my chair, shoulders slumping. "I can't think of anyone that I've talked to that I haven't told you guys—"

Elijah's hand shot out and covered mine. "You're right, Shelby. Someone in law enforcement would have the connections to have been able to kill Kevin. What exactly did you talk about with Deputy Wentz before I arrived on the scene that day?"

"Deputy Wentz?" Jason leaned forward. "Now there's a rat that I could totally see being involved in something like this."

From inside the house, Kodi started yapping like a crazy dog, at the same time as I heard the stomping of footsteps coming through the gardens.

As a unit, we all spun to face the side yard.

The Rat

ELIJAH WAS OUT OF his chair, and shoving me behind him, before I could hardly register the sight of paunchy Deputy Jerry Wentz striding toward us across the lawn—with a huge black gun pointed at us. Jason stepped up by Elijah's side, and Mom stopped next to me and grabbed my hand. We ducked behind the wall of law enforcement for a moment, but then I couldn't help peering around Elijah's shoulder.

Jerry squinted at Jason. "A rat, Undersheriff? I knew you didn't like me, but wasn't sure it went that far."

Jason shifted, broadening his stance. "I guess you're being here is proving my point."

Kodi continued to bark, scratching at the door with all the fury pent up in his little body.

Jerry cast him an irritated glance, and for one heart-stopping moment, I wondered if he would blast my little fur baby away, but he seemed content to see that Kodi couldn't get at him. He returned his attention toward us and caught sight of me peeking out from behind Elijah's arm.

"There you are." His lips thinned into a satisfied smirk.

Elijah nudged me back behind him with his arm. Then he slid his hand beneath the hem of his shirt and my eyes widened as he withdrew a black pistol. He kept his arm bent, the pistol resting against his hip.

"Ah, ah, ah!" Jerry chastised. "Hands where I can see them, please. Both of you!" His volume rose on that last sentence.

I'm still not sure what made me do it, but before Elijah could give up his weapon, I snatched it from his hand. Jerry wouldn't suspect me of having a gun, surely. And if he did, it would only be because of his overactive criminal mind.

Elijah and Jason both raised their hands above their heads.

Dear Lord in heaven! I looked at the black weapon. I had no idea how to use it. If I pointed it at Jerry and pulled the trigger, would it fire? Or was there more I had to do to make it work?

"You didn't just pull a gun from your concealed carry holster?" Jerry's voice was sharp, irritated.

Uh-oh. We were about to lose our only chance at escape from this psycho.

Elijah shrugged. "I'm off duty today. At least I'm supposed to be."

While Elijah spoke, I quickly shoved the gun into my waistband and pulled my sweatshirt down over it.

"Don't play with me, Sheriff. I know you are always packing. Step aside. Now! Ladies, get out here and so help me if either of you are pointing a weapon at me, I'll shoot first. This here rifle will put a hole in you so big that your stupid yappy dog will fit through it."

"Don't shoot," Mom said, thrusting her hands above Jason's shoulder to show they were empty. "We're clean!"

Heart beating in my throat, I followed Mom's lead and showed my hands before stepping around Elijah. I halfway expected crazy Jerry to blow me away without asking questions, but instead he looked first Mom and then me over from head to toe. His glare snapped back to Elijah. "Why did your hand stay behind your back for so long?"

Elijah shrugged. "I was trying to hold my girl's hand, Jerry. Keep her calm." As if to emphasize his point, he reached out and grabbed my hand, lacing his fingers with mine above our heads.

"No! No, no, no. No holding hands. All of you step apart until I can pat you down. Geez, your dog just won't SHUT UP!" He yelled the last command at the glass door that poor Kodi was still madly trying to claw through.

That only made Kodi more frantic to come and help us. He snarled, showing Jerry his teeth.

Jerry ignored him. He swung his rifle at Jason. "You first. All your weapons on the ground. Nice and slow, and then you kick them to me."

Jason gingerly pulled his gun from its holster and set it on the ground. He followed that with a taser, and then Jerry insisted that he remove his holster, and lift each pant-leg so he could make sure he didn't have an ankle holster.

My mouth felt dry and I was beginning to feel a little lightheaded. I couldn't seem to pull my focus from that awful gun in Jerry's hands.

"Calm, Shel. Just breathe calmly."

Elijah's soft voice drew my attention, but he wasn't looking at me. He still had all his attention focused on Jerry.

It was only then that I realized that my breath had been puffing loudly and rapidly. No wonder I was a little lightheaded.

Wait. I could use that to our advantage. But I'd better do it quickly, before Jerry set to patting us down.

Jason dropped his pantleg and stood, hands raised. "That's all, Jerry! No more weapons."

"I'll be the judge of that," Jerry snarled. He scanned Mom up and down and then smirked. "Not much room to hide a weapon in that dress, now is there?"

Jason shifted, expression hard.

Jerry motioned for Mom to spin. She complied.

"I don't feel so good." I stumbled sideways, collapsing against Elijah, like I needed his strength to hold me up. I could only hope he'd realize what I'd done with the gun.

"Stand up!" Jerry snapped, just as I'd hoped he would.

"Please. I just need a minute." I straightened, but stepped in front of Elijah and leaned against him.

"She's not so great in high-pressure situations like this," Elijah offered. He spread his legs, to accept my additional weight, his hands still raised.

"Fine, whatever. Just keep your hands where I can see them, and don't forget this baby is powerful enough that one shot can travel through both of you." He waved his rifle. "You're good, he motioned for Mom to step back beside Jason. Now you, Sheriff."

My heart kicked with wild hope.

Elijah lowered his hands to my shoulders like he was going to move me to one side.

Kodiak went berserk again, drawing an irritated glance from Jerry.

In a flash, Elijah's hand dropped to my waistband. The pistol tugged free.

I lunged to one side.

Jason scooped Mom behind himself.

Elijah fired.

Jerry screamed. Lost his grip on his rifle. Clutched his bleeding hand.

"Hands up, Wentz! Hands up!" Elijah barked.

Jerry whimpered his way through raising his hands, all while trying to stem the bleeding with a pain-weakened grip. "You shot me!"

"You think?" Elijah motioned to me without taking his eyes off of Jerry. "Please get me a kitchen towel or something I can tie around his wrist. Don't want him bleeding out before we get some answers. Jason, pat him down, please."

Jason did, finding nothing.

I couldn't seem to find the strength to move.

"Shelby, please. We have to stop the bleeding."

"Right. Sorry."

"I'll get it." Mom beat me to it. She hurried into the house, lowering a hand to keep Kodi from escaping as she did so.

I dug my feet from the turf, where they'd seemed to bury themselves, and hurried to pull out one of the chairs at the table. "Here, he can sit here. We'll be able to help him better that way."

"Not until you remove all the utensils."

It was only table knives and forks, but I guessed Elijah was simply being super cautious. "Right. On it." I quickly stacked all our plates, dumped all the silverware onto the stack, and then moved to set it on the lawn a few paces away. I didn't want to miss a moment of the conversation that was about to ensue.

"Why are you here, Jerry?" Elijah's voice was hard and held an edge that surprisingly made me feel a little sorry for poor Jerry. "You been running a crime syndicate while working for me?"

His face was pale, and sweat dotted his forehead. He looked like he could pass out at any second.

"Table's ready," I said.

Elijah motioned with his pistol for Jerry to sit just as Mom returned with our first-aid kit.

"I've got it," Jason said, taking the kit from her. "I don't want you anywhere near him." He nudged her toward me.

Mom came to stand by me on the lawn.

Jason withdrew a roll of gauze and motioned for Jerry to hold out his injured hand.

I crinkled my nose and looked away. I settled a hand over my stomach, willing my crepes to stay where I'd put them.

Mom wrapped an arm around me and pulled me close.

"What are you doing here, Jerry?" Elijah repeated.

"I need a doctor!"

"The faster you talk to me, the faster I'll call you a doctor."

I flashed Elijah a look. Was he allowed to do that? Even Jason looked up from where he was cinching the tourniquet around Jerry's wrist.

"Talk to me, Jerry. Start with what it is you think Shelby knows." Elijah sank into the chair across the table from the injured deputy, gun still held at the ready.

"The name of my boss."

Jason stepped back from the injured limb and Jerry cradled it against his chest with a wince.

All eyes turned toward me.

I touched my fingertips to my chest. "I have no idea what he's talking about. I don't know any names of anyone."

Jerry narrowed his gaze. "But they said his name when they were on the boat."

"You mean the guy they said was going to be really unhappy about the loss of the diamonds?" I shook my head. "I didn't catch the name. The marina was too loud, and the wind kicked up at that point too."

Jerry searched my features. "You really don't know?"

I leaned forward. "I'm telling you, I have no idea!"

Elijah tapped the table with the gun to draw Jerry's attention. "You've been after her because you thought she overheard someone's name?"

Jerry nodded, still searching my face.

"Is it Aaron King?" Elijah prodded.

Jerry barked a laugh and then winced. "Aaron King? Not a chance. He's just a wannabe."

"Who is it, Jerry? We'll protect you."

Jerry huffed. "Like you protected Kevin Swift?"

Elijah leaned across the table, his penetrating gaze drilling into Jerry. "Was that you that shot him?"

Jerry sagged against his chair. "Yes. But he has other crack shots besides me. If I talk to you, I'm done for."

"I'll take you to Seattle, right now."

Jerry shook his head. "Not far enough." Jerry started shaking. Like really shaking. His head lolled to one side. "Not . . . feeling . . . so good." His words were slightly slurred.

Mom gasped. "His blood pressure is tanking!"

Jason and Elijah exchanged a look.

As Jerry started to slide from his chair, Jason leapt forward and caught him. Jerry's eyes rolled back into his head and Jason looked over at Elijah. "I don't think he's faking this." He laid Jerry out carefully on our patio.

Mom hurried over and raised his booted feet onto one of our patio chairs.

Elijah sighed and slumped against the table, but then immediately straightened and snatched up his phone. He dialed and held it to his ear for a moment, before saying, "Yeah, this is Sheriff Elijah Gains. I need an ambulance immediately at 7323 Heron Lane in Cobalt Bay. A man's been shot and he just passed out."

Carrot Cake and Amazing Kisses

ELIJAH RETURNED LATER THAT evening just after I'd checked in our two guests. I kept the curtains to the back yard closed, so they wouldn't see the crime-scene tape cordoning off the area where Elijah had shot his deputy. Because it was an officer-involved shooting, an investigator from Anacortes was slated to arrive the next day to conduct the investigation.

Elijah informed me that Mom and I would likely have to answer some questions.

I motioned for him to follow me into the kitchen and sliced him off a large piece of the carrot cake Mom had stress-baked that afternoon. "Are you in danger of losing your job?"

"I don't think so." He dallied his fork through the cream cheese frosting as I set a large glass of milk beside him. "Jason concurs. It was a clean shoot, especially since there were civilians to protect."

I gave a little bow. "Happy to be of service."

He smiled and took a bite of cake. "Oh, wow." He pointed his fork at the remainder on his plate. "That's good."

"I know, right? But let's face it, there isn't much that Mom makes that I don't like." I smiled.

"You're not having any?"

I pressed my lips together. "I *might* have already had two pieces this afternoon."

His gaze drifted the length of me before dropping to his cake.

I looked down at myself. I felt like I looked pretty presentable today in a gypsy skirt and peasant blouse in matching seashore blues. "What?"

He shook his head. "I was just wondering how you stay so trim."

Trim? Was that a compliment? Or was that a description that someone might give of say . . . Olive Oyl, the cartoon girl from *Popeye*?

I must have pulled a face of some kind because when I looked back at Elijah, he was grinning at me across the island counter.

"It was a compliment, Shel. I might be just a little out of practice with giving them."

"Oh." I felt the warmth of pleasure in my cheeks. "I was just wondering because you know, I was told I could pass for homeless just a few days ago, and that sort of sticks with a girl."

He chuckled. "Speaking of Jerry. He came out of surgery fine. And I'm thankful he's going to continue to have use of his hand. He's been arrested, of course, for his confession to killing Kevin Swift."

"And Kirk is slated for trial for the murder of Anthony Moretti?"

He nodded. "And we also solved the pet-scam case. So I guess that's a wrap on three cases this week. Which looks good on the books." He sighed and toyed with his cake.

I rested my forearms on the counter and leaned toward him. "So why is it you don't look too happy?"

He tossed down the fork and twisted his milk glass instead. "I just don't like to think of another criminal out there somewhere. One who is apparently terrifying enough to scare Jerry silent."

I reached over and laid my hand on top of his. "Take the win, E. Three wins, in fact. Besides, no crime happened that you are aware of with whoever this other guy that Jerry talked about is—he didn't even get the diamonds he wanted—so you wouldn't be able to make any arrests anyhow, right?"

"That's true. As far as we know." He frowned.

"Isn't there a verse in the Bible that says something like 'each day has enough trouble of its own'?"

His frown softened as his gaze met mine. "There is."

"Great. So . . ." I spread my hands. "Problem solved." I offered him a cheesy grin.

He chuckled. "And there's amazing carrot cake too."

"There is. And maybe even a comedy movie in the family room with a girl who is trim?"

He tilted his head, eyes sparkling like the waves of the Pacific just before sunset. "Is she going to let a certain sheriff put his arm around her?"

I tapped a finger to my lips like I was really having to think hard about that. But I have to tell you that anticipation nearly stripped all the strength from my knees. Thankfully, I had the counter to lean on. "She just might at that."

"Then I'm in."

He pushed his cake to one side and leaned forward to press a gentle kiss to my lips. "I'm glad God brought you to Cobalt Bay, Shel."

I smiled. "Me too."

I was even more glad of it when we sank into the cushions of the comfy loveseat in the family room and I settled against the sturdy warmth of Elijah's side with his arm encircling me.

I must have drifted off at some point in the movie because when I awoke later, I'd missed part of it. I stretched and yawned.

Elijah must have fallen asleep too? I turned to look at him and that was when I realized that he was no longer beside me. I frowned. Grabbed my phone from the table in front of me to check the time. Had I been so sound asleep that he'd left without saying goodbye? No. It couldn't be, because only about fifteen minutes had passed.

Maybe he'd just needed to use the restroom. I stayed where I was, watching the familiar scenes flow across the screen, and lamenting the loss of his warmth and closeness. But after a few minutes, I realized that he really should be back by now.

I stood and went to check the restroom just down the hall. The door was open and no one was inside.

Strange. I wandered back to the kitchen. Elijah's keys were still on the island where he'd put them when he'd sat down to have cake. A check of the driveway showed that his truck was still out there too.

My heart started to thump with a little concern.

I whipped out my phone and dialed him, but the phone only rang through to his voice message.

I hurried back to search through the two rooms I shared with Mom. He wasn't there. And a perusal of the upstairs and back garden also didn't reveal him.

I paused on the patio trying to think where else to look. The problem was, I couldn't think of any other logical places to check. My pulse pounded in earnest now. What in the world?

"Shelby?" Mom spoke from just behind me.

I gasped and spun toward her.

"What is it, hon? You look terrified."

"Mom? I think Elijah has gone missing."

"Gone missing? Whatever do you mean?"

"I mean, one minute he was here. I fell asleep for fifteen minutes, and when I woke up, he's nowhere to be found, but his keys and his truck are still here! I tried to call and got no answer."

"Shelby Lynn, he has to be here. You've just missed him somehow. Just calm down. I'll help you find him."

Mom proceeded to check all the places I'd just checked. She also looked in the garage, but Elijah was nowhere to be found. We took flashlights and spent fifteen minutes searching the grounds. We met back up under the porch light on the patio.

"Land almighty, Shelby," Mom gasped. "I think you better call Jason."

With trembling fingers, I did just that.

I scanned the yard once more as I waited for Jason to answer. Empty.

Jason's voice was sleepy when he picked up on the fifth ring. "Undersheriff White."

"Jason? Sorry to call so late. I think you'd better come to the B&B right away. Elijah is missing." I collapsed into the patio chair even as I said the words.

Where in the world could he have gone? My thoughts flashed to the feelings that had flooded me just after Daddy passed, and I gulped as I realized I was feeling the same emotions now. Not again! *Jesus, please. I don't think I can go through something like this again!*

Quick as a flash, a verse similar to the one I'd shared with Elijah less than an hour and a half ago flashed through my mind. *Do not be anxious about anything, but in every situation, by prayer and petition, with thanksgiving, present your requests to God.*

I swallowed. *Lord, I'm going to be a failure at obeying the "do not be anxious" part of that verse. Please forgive me and help me to do better at trusting You. But mostly, wherever Elijah is, please keep him safe and don't let anything bad happen to him!*

It didn't feel like enough, but it was the only thing I could think to do that would help at the moment. I stayed right where I was and kept right on praying, doing my best to squash my anxiety.

And failing pretty miserably.

About Trinity Colt

Author Trinity Colt grew up as a third-culture-kid. She has survived killer bees, poisonous snakes, charging buffalos, and boarding school cafeteria food. She has raised four kids and now has one grand-child. She divides her time between church activities, running three businesses, entertaining her petulant Pomeranian, keeping the house livable and those in it fed, and publishing humorous cozy mystery stories that capture her zest for life.

Find out more about Trinity Colt at TrinityColt.com.

Crepes

Crepe is French for pancake. However crepes are very thin and cook up really fast. They are delicious and can be filled with just about anything your heart desires.

Ingredients

1 ½ cups of milk
1 cup all-purpose flour
2 eggs
1 tablespoon cooking oil
1 – 2 tablespoons sugar
Dash of salt

Combine all ingredients in a bowl and mix until combined into a runny batter. Heat a non-stick 8 to 12 inch skillet (size of pan doesn't really matter) with oil to medium heat. Ladle about 4 to 6 tablespoons of batter into the middle and quickly swirl the pan to spread the batter into a wide circle. Fry it until the top just starts to lose its gloss, then flip with a pancake turner and let it cook for another moment until the underside is browned. Remove from pan and repeat until all batter is cooked, adding more oil to the pan, as necessary.

Fill with any of your favorite fillings. Fruit, peanut butter, Nutella, or blintz. (See super easy recipe next page.)

Blintz Filling

Blintz filling is a sweet cheesy bite of deliciousness that you simply have to try!

Ingredients

1 8oz block cream cheese warmed to room temperature.
2 teaspoons sour cream
1.5 – 2 cups of powdered sugar
1 tsp vanilla

Mix all ingredients with a rotary mixer. It should be the consistency of thick frosting. Lay a crepe on your plate. Spoon 2-3 tablespoons of blintz down the middle of the crepe and roll the crepe up like a sleeping bag. Top with your favorite sliced fruit like strawberries or raspberries.

Made in the USA
Columbia, SC
28 October 2024